"The [herald] of a new literary renaissance . . . [The] so-called bourgeoisie will regurgitate over Mr. Anderson's stories. They'll want to say ''Taint so!' But it is so, and the only reason the bourgeoisie will object is because Mr. Anderson has drawn our picture for everybody (including white folks; in fact, mostly white folks) to see. There's the rub."

—P. L. Prattis, *Pittsburgh Courier*

"What distinguishes Alston's stories from the usual white American variety—derived from O. Henry at however far a remove—is that there's no inevitable whip-crack ending. In fact, he makes his points by judicious 'signifying' . . . We see [his subject] clearly from the part of the retina that has not been fogged by too much direct staring."

—Robert Graves

"Now tender, now violent, touched equally with poetry and irony."

—Gene Baro, *New York Herald Tribune*

"In spite of some strong themes, [these stories] are told with a rare delicacy, by what Mr. Anderson calls signifying rather than direct statement; they have no tricks and yet how clever they are . . . I do not remember a small book which has given me such a large experience."

—Rumer Godden

LOVER MAN

ALSTON ANDERSON

WITH AN AFTERWORD BY

KINOHI NISHIKAWA

McNally Editions

New York

McNally Editions
52 Prince St., New York 10012

ISBN: 978-1-946022-54-7
E-book: 978-1-946022-55-4

Design by Jonathan Lippincott

1   3   5   7   9   10   8   6   4   2

For Marshall, with thanks

CONTENTS

LOVER MAN

THE CHECKER BOARD

'James? James, you out there? Lord, I wonder where that nigger is now. James?'

'I'm right here,' my father said.

'You come on in this house before I hit you up side the head. You get the corn like I asked you to?'

'Yeah, I got it.'

'And the bread? I bet you anything in the world you done forgot the bread. You get the bread, James?'

'Yeah, I got the bread.'

My father picked up the corn and the bread and went inside the house. We'd been playing checkers, with him sitting on a bench on the front porch, the checker board on a chair, and me squatting on the floor on the other side. I could hear him dump the corn on the table in the kitchen; and then the paper rattled as my mother took the bread out of it. I looked at the checker board and thought: If I move that piece right there he'll have to jump it then I can move that one up and get me a king. I could hear my father coming back out to the porch. When he got to the doorway my mother said, 'James?'

My father stopped. 'Yes, Mary-Jane.'

'You cut the wood like I asked you?'

'I cut some last night, Mary-Jane.'

'That ain't nearbout enough and you know it. You go on out there and cut me some wood.'

My father came out on the porch and stood looking down at the checker board. The muscles in his jaw always moved when he was thinking about something, and they were moving now. He leaned over the board and put his hands on his knees, but he didn't sit down. He looked at the pieces, studying them; then he moved. He jumped three of my men at once, bing-bing-bing. 'Hot *damn*,' I said, and scratched my head.

'Didn't see that, did you?'

'No, sir, I sure didn't.'

I moved, and he countered it. My mother came out on the porch with both hands at her hips.

'You mean to tell me you can stand up there and play checkers with that child when I done asked you to do something? You's the laziest man I seen yet, I swear before God in heaven.' She went into the front room. 'Ask the man to do something and he act just like I ain't said boo. After I done worked and slaved in this house all day it look like the *least* you could do is have some kind of consideration for the things I got to put up with.' She was in the kitchen now, talking louder. 'That other no-good son of yours is up there in that pool hall gambling and that no-count bitch of a daughter of yours is up there up North making a whore of herself.' She started to cry. 'Lord have mercy, I don't know *what* I done to deserve this. If I had it to do all over again I'd marry a white man. You don't believe it? A nigger ain't worth nothing a-tall on God's earth, just as sure as I'm His witness.'

'Your move,' my father said. He sat down on the bench. The muscles in his jaw were still moving, but he didn't have nary an expression on his face. I moved a piece from the back row. 'Watch this one,' he said, and pointed to a piece I'd left exposed. I thanked him and put back the one I'd moved. I covered the piece my father had pointed to and as I did my mother came out on the porch again.

'James, you going do like I asked you?'

'Mary-Jane, I'm going do it just as soon as I'm through here. Now let me be.'

'You shouting at me again, nigger? I done told you a million times *never* to shout at me. I'm a *lady*, you hear me? Soon's you get that through that thick head of yours the better it'll be for all of us. Now you git on out there in that yard and cut the wood like I asked you to.'

My father looked up at her. I don't mean to say 'up at her'; just 'up'. Because even sitting down like he was my father was nearbout as tall as she is standing up. I could hear him laughing to himself. He shook his head from side to side and got up, real slow-like. He went down in the yard and then around to the back of the house. My mother went inside, and I could hear her bustling around in the kitchen. She was slamming things around and muttering to herself: 'No-count, no-good . . . work and slave all day. . . .' Then I could hear my father chopping wood. He always hummed the same tune when he was chopping wood, and swung the axe in time to it: Hmmm-hmmm-hmmm-hmmm-CHACK! Hmmm-hmmm-hmmm-hmmm-CHACK!

When he was through he came around the side of the house with an armful of wood. I ran down from the porch and took some from him, and we went inside the house together. My mother was blowing at the fire in the stove, and the kitchen was full of smoke. We dumped the wood on the floor beside the stove and went out on the porch and finished the checker game. He won.

By the time my brother got home that evening we were sitting down at the dinner table. My mother was dishing out the food. There was a lot of steam coming up from the platter, and every once in a while she'd frown and move her head away. I had my eye on a nice big piece of fatback that was sitting right on top of the greens. When my mother helped my plate she moved the spoon all around it, but she didn't give it to me. Thomas, my brother, sat down without saying good evening. As soon as his plate was in front of him he started eating.

'Ain't you going say grace?' my mother said. 'You act just like you was bring up in a pig-pen.' My brother stopped eating and looked at her. He put his knife and fork down and said, 'Gracious Father we thank thee—'

'You stop!' my mother said. 'Can't you see I ain't finished serving yet? James, when you going teach these children some manners?'

'What you been up to?' my father said to Thomas.

'I been over at Miss Florence's.'

'You're a lie, my mother said. 'You been up there at that pool hall all day, that's where you been.'

'What you been doing?' my father said.

'Making a bookshelf,' my brother said.

'Say the grace, James,' my mother said.

'She pay you for it?' my father said.

'James, I said say the grace,' my mother said.

'She give me five dollars,' my brother said.

'Only five?' my father said.

'James?' my mother said. 'You hear what I said?'

'Gracious Father who art in Heaven we thank Thee for this food which we are about to receive for Christ's sake amen,' my father said. 'Only five?'

'You mean to tell me you's the deacon of the church and you say grace like that?' my mother said. 'Take your foot off that chair, Aaron.'

'It wasn't worth no more than that,' my brother said.

'How big was it?' my father said.

'Six by five,' Thomas said.

'Aaron, take your foot off that chair, I said,' my mother said. I took my foot off the chair. 'James, when you going get that child some shoes?'

'That wasn't too bad,' my father said.

'Mutton Head ain't got no shoes neither,' I said.

'He don't need none right now,' my father said.

'You hush,' my mother said to me. 'Don't need none? You mean to tell me you going let that child start school in September without shoes?'

'He'll have some by then,' my father said.

'Mutton Head ain't got—'

'Hush!' my mother said.

If I made a king I'd have whupped him.

'Yeah,' my mother said. 'I know. He'll have them shoes just like I had my anniversary present this year.'

'Mary-Jane, you going bring that up *again*?'

'I'm going bring it up long as I please. I'm going bring it up 'til you learns that you's got some 'sponsibilities in this world besides the Bible and corn liquor.'

'Jesus, good sweet Christ,' my father said.

'Pass the salt,' my brother said.

Maybe next time I can make three kings.

'You better get that child some shoes right soon, that's all I got to say,' my mother said.

'Pass the salt,' my brother said.

'Don't you be yelling at me, boy,' my mother said.

'Can't you leave nobody in peace?' my father said.

'Pass the salt!' my brother said, real loud. I reached way over and got the cup the salt was in and handed it to him.

'James, you going sit there and let that boy yell at me like that? What's the matter? You scared of him now that he's big as you? Is that it? Git up and wash your hands, Thomas, 'fore you salt God's food with your nasty fingers. Is that it? You scared of your own son?'

My father sighed and didn't say a word. My brother kept on salting the food with his fingers.

'Thomas, you hear what I said? You git on up and wash your hands 'fore I slap you up side the head.'

'Yeah, woman,' Thomas said, 'and that'll be the last time you slap anybody, I swear.'

'Hush, Tom,' my father said, real soft-like.

'What's the matter? You scared of your own son?' my mother said.

'Mutton Head's way bigger than me,' I said, 'but I ain't scared of him.'

'Hush!' my father said, but he looked like he was about to laugh.

'You hear the ball scores today?' my brother said.

'The Yankees won,' I said.

'That all you two got to talk about?' my mother said.

'I ain't studying the Yankees,' Thomas said. 'What'd the Dodgers do?'

'They lost,' I said. 'The Cards beat 'em six-two.' My brother frowned and I said, 'Don't nobody root for bums but bums, noway.' He hit at me and I ducked and laughed.

'Don't you be hitting at that child,' my mother said.

'Jesus Christ, Mary-Jane, can't you leave nobody in peace? They won't doing nothing but playing,' my father said.

'James, I done told you one time today not to yell at me,' my mother said. 'That's all you ever done since the day you married me twenty-four years ago last June 3rd.'

'June 4th,' my father said.

'All you ever do is yell, yell, yell,' my mother said. She got to crying. 'And all I ever do in this Godforsaken house all day is work, work, work. I ain't only got the house to clean and food to fix and y'all's clothes to wash, but other people's clothes to wash, too. God knows what I ever done to deserve this. And you gallavanting around with these young gals. Don't think I don't know it, James Jessup!' She got to dabbing at her eyes with her apron, but she was still crying. 'A man ain't good for nothing in this whole world but to get a woman children and trouble.'

My father got up from the table and went inside the bedroom. My brother got up and went out on the porch. I could hear him pulling the bench out so's he could set his feet up on it like he always did. My mother started clearing the table. Underneath the light her face looked like it was dark blue, and her eyes were red.

'Don't cry, Mamma,' I said. She didn't say anything. I got up and helped her with the dishes, then I went inside and went to bed.

If I got that king I could've whupped him.

The next morning when I got up my brother was already gone. I didn't know what it was that woke me at first; then I heard. It was my mother calling out 'James? Lord have mercy. James? James? Jesus God in heaven. James? James? . . .'

THE DOZENS

One day me and Mutton Head was walking through the woods on the way to a creek. The sun was shining through the pine trees and sometimes I would be in the shade and then in the sun again, quick-like. Other times I would look at Mutton Head's back and it would be just like he was walking past one of them Venetian blinds when it's dark inside and the street light comes shining through. Mutton Head was two years older than me, but he was short and thick and somebody said one time that he had a head like a mutton chop. So we called him Mutton Head, but his real name was James Washington.

When we got to the creek it was dark. It wasn't *real* dark. What I mean is the sun had got covered up by a cloud, and it looked like it might rain some later on. But since it was the onliest cloud in the sky neither one of us was thinking of going back home or nothing. It just seem like the cloud was there, like a homen. It made me feel funny-like. When we set down on the bank we could see a piece o' straw floating slow-like on top of the muddy water. Now that I come to think of it seem like that was a homen, too.

'That there straw sure look like a boat, don't it?' Mutton Head said. When I said yeah he said, 'A man tell me one time peoples used to be buried in them things.'

'In a *boat*?'

'Uh-huh.'

'Nobody can't be buried in no boat,' I said.

'I didn't mean they was buried, fool. I just mean when somebody died they'd put the body in a boat and let the boat float down the river. Come on, gimme a worm.'

I took a worm from the tin can I was carrying and give it to him. The straw had done floated further downstream a ways, and I watched it drift slow-like against the bank on the other side. It stopped. When Mutton Head put the worm on the hook I could see it get right red at the tip end, but it didn't squirm. Mutton Head got up so's he could get more distant and threw the line out fur as he could. Then he set down again.

'Set the can 'tween us so's I can get to it,' he said. I set the can between us and when I did I could feel the edge of it sharp against my thumb. For a long time didn't neither one of us catch a thing.

'Boy, boy, I sure would like to get some o' that,' Mutton Head said. He was always talking about getting some. I looked across to the other side to see who it was he was talking about this time, but there won't nobody over there. In fact, we hadn't seen a living soul for going on two hours.

'Some o' what?' I said.

'*You* know who I'm talking 'bout,' he said, and laughed. 'Hmph, hmph, hmph,' he said.

'Some o' what?' I said.

He spat into the creek and we both watched the bubbles float downstream and disappear. The sun came out just then and setting in the sudden light his skin looked like a Nestlé milkbar. 'Sheeit,' he said. 'You wouldn't know what I'm talking 'bout noways. You's just a kid, tall and skinny as you is.'

'Some o' what?' I said.

'Maybelle,' he said.

Maybelle was my play mother. She was seventeen, and when she walked you could see her body moving from side to side underneath her dress, like when you shake rice in a strainer. Everybody said Maybelle had real fine hair, just like a Hawaiian. Mutton Head knowed good and well I didn't like him to talk about Maybelle that way.

'Yeah, *boy*!' he said. 'You sure done gone and got yourself just 'bout the finest play mother in town.'

'Hell,' I said. 'Your own mother ain't so bad herself.'

He pushed me real rough and said, 'Look out, nigger! I done told you I don' play the dozens.'

'Well, quit talking 'bout my play mother,' I said.

'It ain't the same thing, fool.'

'How come it ain't?'

'You mean you love Maybelle just like your *own* mother?'

'No, I reckon not.'

'Well, awright then. It ain't the same thing.'

He was still mad. I was sorry I put him in the dozens, but he talked about my play mother, didn't he? Mutton Head didn't never play the dozens with nobody, not even me, his ace-cut. We didn't talk for a good while after that. Every so often he would hold his pole up so that the line came out of the water, with the hook wet and shiny and the worm red on the tip end of it; then he'd let it down in the water again, jerky-like. He was mad, alright; and I was mad at myself for slipping him in the dozens. 'Hell,' I said, and kicked at the water.

'She a fine chick anyway,' Mutton Head said after a while, 'even if she *is* your play mammy.' He looked at me and laughed.

'Hell,' I said. And then I laughed too, and everything was alright.

We used to go fishing every Saturday, Mutton Head and me. One time Pee Wee used to come with us, but he done got too old to go fishing, he said, so he shoots pool and sometimes he shoots crap in back of the poolroom. Pee Wee is my older brother. He's the best dancer in town. When he dance everybody stops and stand around and watch. Most times they clap their hands in time to the music and sometimes somebody says, 'Ooooh-wee! *Look* at that nigger go!' Then around ten or ten-thirty he comes over to me and says, 'Look-a-here, Lil One, ain't it about time you be getting some sleep?' And I go home and write me a letter to Maybelle and slip it to her next Monday in school. Sometimes I copy me part of a poem from a book and put it in, but she don't never know the difference. When school is out she be standing outside with some other girls and when I pass by she says, 'Hey, Lil One, that was a real nice letter.' And she turns to her friends, with her hair falling black down her back, and says, 'That there's my new play son.' And I look in her eyes and we both know.

The cloud was way off in the distant now and the sun had done got real hot. Mutton Head got up and went a little ways out in the creek and started to washing one foot with the other. The sole of his foot was yellower than mine, because he was darker. I told him to get back up on the bank because maybe a moccasin or something but he said 'Hell' and stood out there anyway.

'You going to the dance tonight?'

'I don't reckon so,' I said.

'How come you ain't . . . 'cause Maybelle ain't going be there?'

'I reckon 'cause I ain't got a mind to.'

'Aw, nigger, you know you're lying.'

'Maybe I am and maybe I ain't.'

He turned around, then, and looked at me. He was getting mad again, and so was I. 'Think you're cute, don't you?' he said.

'Maybe I am and maybe I ain't,' I said. 'But I know who *is* right cute.'

He dropped his fishing pole, then, and splashed out of the creek and next thing I knew he had me pinned down on the bank and his face was right close to mine.

'You skinny black son of a bitch,' he said. 'Who's cute? Who? Tell me so I can break your God damn neck. Who's cute?' His breath smelled like fatback and collard greens, and I could feel his fingernails in my shoulders.

'I won't talking 'bout your mother,' I said. 'Turn me loose, Mutton Head.'

He hauled off and slapped me, hard. I was about to cry, but I held it back. He called me a real bad name and I said,

'I won't talking 'bout your mother, Mutton Head, honest to God I won't.'

'Who, then?'

'Maybelle, Mutton Head, I was talking 'bout Maybelle.'

'You're a black lie.'

'No I ain't, Mutton Head. I swear 'fore God I ain't.'

I knew good and well that he knew I was lying, and I could tell from the expression on his face that he knew I knowed it. He turned me aloose anyway; leastways he turned my shoulders aloose, but he was still bending over me. I could see the muscles working in his jaw, like he was gritting and ungritting his teeth. His breath was coming right fast. Lying there I got to noticing little things about him I'd never noticed before, like the fact that he had a mole on the right side of his neck and the fact that his eyes won't black, like I thought, but dark brown.

'I ain't lying, Mutton Head,' I said. 'Here's my right hand to God I ain't.'

He stood up, then, and walked back into the creek. The back of his shirt was torn. I set there on the bank watching him kick at the water and curse. He had his hands to his hips. I set there rubbing the sting on my face, numb-like, trying to figure out whether his shirt was tore all the time and I hadn't noticed it or whether he tore it when he grabbed me. All of a sudden he said, 'Hot damn, Miss Blue! My *pole*!'

I didn't have no idea how far his pole had done floated by this time, but I didn't care, either. I was thinking about the fact that my best friend had done hit me, and it was then I realized I was crying. 'Muttonchop bastard,' I said, and wiped the tear away.

In a little while I wasn't mad any more. I got to thinking about the dance that night, and about what I'd say to Mutton Head when he got back: 'I reckon I'll go to the dance after all, Mutton Head.' 'Sure 'nough?' 'Yeah, I reckon I will.' He'd pick up his pole, then, and I'd pick up mine and we'd start out for home. 'And I won't put you in the dozens any more, Mutton Head. I swear 'gainst my name, I won't.' 'OK, Lil One,' he'd say, and rub my head like he like to do.

I could see the dancehall, too, with niggers packed inside it tighter than goosepimples. I could see my brother dancing and people clapping, jumping to Jimmie Lunceford. Then I could see me in the centre of the crowd, instead of my brother, and I could hear people say 'Go, Lil One, *go*!' when I danced with Maybelle, with her titties bobbing up and down and hair flying.

Then I heard it. It seem like he'd done gone a long, long ways, because I just barely could hear it: 'Lillll Wawnnn! . . .'

I set my fishing pole down and jumped up. I didn't know what Mutton Head wanted, but I could tell from the sound of his voice that it was real urgent. I didn't like walking in the water—and still don't—because I always like to know what I'm walking on. I looked alongside the bank of the creek for a path, but there wasn't none. I jumped in the water and started splashing downstream. 'Damn fool,' I said out loud. 'I *told* him to stay on the bank.' By this time I thought I knew what it was: a snake. 'Damn fool,' I said again, splashing downstream. Then I stumbled and stopped short, like a soldier when he gets hit by a bullet. 'Jesus Christ,' I said. 'Sweet Jesus Christ.'

Because then I remembered. We never seen it, neither of us, but every living soul in town had done told us about it. Old Man Maypeck told us about it first. When I started downstream again, with my heart beating like a bass drum, I could see Old Man Maypeck standing on his front porch telling us about it, standing there in that black suit he wore every day God sent with a stiff-collar white shirt and a red polka-dot scarf and a malacca cane. Quicksand.

'Lillll Wawnnn! . . .'

'I'm coming!' I yelled back. My voice didn't sound like my own. I started running again, and it seem to me like every step I took the mud at the bottom of the creek got softer and softer I thought: Maybe it ain't the quicksand after all. Maybe he done got hisself bit by a snake; and if it's a snake the best thing to do right quick is . . . but I got holes in my back teeth and then we'd both be dead and gone. It's quicksand that's what it is. You know good and well it's quicksand. *Fool*, I *told* him to stay on the bank. A rope, that's what I need. It ain't quicksand, it's a snake. A great long rope like my mother's clothesline. Get something he can get aholt to, fool. Get. . . .

'Lillll Wawnnn! . . .'

I seen him, then. There was a sharp bend in the creek and when I got around it I could see him. It was quicksand, alright. Mutton Head was nearbout up to his waist in it. I seen him struggling, with his fishpole lying yellow in the mud not two feet away from him. I remembered what Old Man Maypeck had said about struggling in quicksand so I yelled out, 'Don't move, James!' and it hit me that that was the first time I ever called him by his real name. 'Don't move!'

I jumped out the creek and on to the bank, and for a split minute my mind went blanker than an eight-o'clock blackboard. Then I took aholt to the limb of a small pine tree and even while I was twisting it I knew that it wouldn't be nearbout long enough. I twisted it off anyway, feeling right hopeful and right helpless all at the same time. When I got back to a place in the creek where I could see him Mutton Head didn't look panicky or nothing. He was looking around him just like a little boy who's got hisself tied up in a ball of loose thread and who's trying to figure out how he got into that mess in the first place. Then he seen me. He reach out for the branch I was holding, even though we was still a good fifteen feet apart and the branch couldn't have been more than three feet long, I swear. I inched closer and closer towards him, holding the branch out fur as I could. The mud was up past his waist now. I could feel myself sinking, or thought I could, so I jumped back and when I did I fell. I jumped up in a panic and scrambled back upstream and on to the bank. I was trembling. I saw a limb on a tall pine that I thought might reach him if I could break it off, so I climbed the tree right quick and got to twisting the limb with all my strength. It broke. I twisted it and twisted it until it came loose, then I jumped clean down to the ground with it and ran back to the creek. Mutton Head was up to his armpits by now, and from where I was I could see his eyes. I never will forget those wild, wide eyes. But he won't saying a word; just reaching out for the branch. I inched up and inched up towards him, careful not to go as fur as I done the time before. I stretched out the branch with both hands—it was right heavy—and he got aholt to it. I started pulling, moving back, back, back . . . then the pine needles slipped out his fingers and he fell face down. I stretched out the branch again, praying with all my heart. He was up to his chin now. He caught aholt to the tip-end of the branch, but lost it again. Then he was gone, gone, with his hands still reaching out for the branch.

Since that day I don't play the dozens no more, and whenever I hear anybody playing them I leave the room.

SIGNIFYING

Women are the most unpredictable things on the face of God's earth. Take Miss Florence, for an instant. We'd done knowed each other for going on eight months, yet there we was: me with a teacup balanced on my knees like I was a Englishman, she sitting on the couch with her back so straight that if you saw only her upper half you'd swear she was sitting on a horse.

'Would you like some more tea?'

I said no thanks. What I needed, then and after, was a drink. But lemme tell you 'bout it.

Like I said, it had done taken us a long time to get to the tea-drinking stage. This despite the fact that her house was less than two blocks from where I live. Yeah, she was a strange one, alright. Schoolteacher. Come down from Philadelphia. Tall woman, slender, small breasted but kinda big hipped, thirty-one or two by this time. Nearbout every single man in town had done tried to get close to her. But she kept her distant. And Pops, I'm here to tell you that that's pretty close to a miracle, because the mens in my town ain't wolves, Jackson, them is *were*wolves, hongry as they is for women. It tickled me to watch them try. First it was Mr Thomas Love: unh-unh. Then James Turner: no, sir. When the single ones won't getting nowheres the married ones took to trying their hands: unh-unh. Even Old Man Maypeck got a gleam in his eye, and took to dropping by right casual-like with flowers: no siree, Bob.

The difference between me and them was that I had done planned me a campaign. I was smart, alright. But things sure'n hell didn't turn out the way I thought they would.

The way I had it figured, I'd treat her just like she treat me. With the difference that I'd let her know from the jump that I was interested, but in a way so's it wouldn't come to her that I *was* till long after I'd done dropped my little hint. Pops, that's a *art*. You can't be practising it on no pretty women, though, because a pretty woman knows you's interested long before you even *sees* her. I calls the technique I used on Miss Florence Tactiful Approach Number One For Ugly Women. But she won't ugly, what I mean. She won't no Lena Horne, but she won't ugly neither. But the way she was acting she may's *well* have been, so I decided to use Number One.

One day I was standing outside the barbershop with some of the boys. Miss Florence come by on her way home from the schoolhouse, and they got to signifying:

'Mmmmm-*mph*! What a fine day *this* is!'

'Yes, Lawd, it sho is.'

'My, my, what a *purty* day!'

'How do, Miss Florence!'

'How do you do.'

'Yes Lawd, I'd sleep in the streets fawdy days and fawdy nights for a day like *that*!'

'Y'all hush your signifying,' I said. 'That there's a *lady*, and 1 won't have y'all signifying 'bout her like that.'

I said it in a tone of voice that wasn't loud, but I knew she heard it. Next time I seen her she had a nice little smile for me, but I acted just like nothing had ever happened.

That was about two weeks after she come to town. After that I would see her in the street and we would speak, but that was all.

Now, I'm a carpenter by trade, and that's how I first got into Miss Florence's house. Said she wanted a bookshelf made, and somebody'd done told her I could make it. She lived in a small house she'd rented from Inez Turner. Won't but a living-room, bedroom, kitchen and bath to the place, but she'd done fixed it up real nice. God knows what she wanted with another bookshelf. She already had two. Anyways, I got to installing this other one in her living-room one Saturday afternoon. I knowed good and well it won't the time to try anything, so I didn't have no intentions or nothing like that. But I notice she couldn't sit still. Kept moving 'bout the room, straightening out things that was already straight, picking up this and moving that. One time I looked up from what I was doing and there she was, standing right side of me. I tended to my business and didn't say nothing.

'I think that's just fine,' she said.

I stood up. 'I'm glad you like it.'

'Do you read much?

'Read?'

She was standing right close to me then, and I noticed that her eyes were real pretty. She had freckles on her face, but you couldn't see them till you got right up close. Cute little nose she had, too, and she didn't wear much lipstick. I noticed all this while I was trying to figure out what she was getting at with this reading business, and what I'd tell her. I didn't think she gave a good damn whether I read or not; figured she was stalling for time or something. But I was wrong. When I told her no, I didn't, she went into a long rigamarole about education and the uplift of the race' or something like that. I got out of there in a hurry.

That was when I decided to drop Number One. To hell with it, y'understand? Next thing you know this woman would have me going to church, or we'd get married and go and live in Philadelphia. And who the hell wants to live in Philadelphia? Or get married, for that matter. So, like I said, to hell with it. She could go jump in a creek and take her uplift with 'er.

But in spite of everything I got to liking the woman. Not in no special way or anything like that, but I liked her. It seemed like we saw one another a lot more on the street after that bookshelf business, and each time she'd have a little something to say. But I kept my distant. So when she invited me to this tea thing I figured there'd be other people there.

Wrong again.

She had her a little victrola, one o' them wind-up ones, and after we'd eliminated the fact that it don't get as hot in Philadelphia as it do in Alabama she started to winding it up. I offered to help her, but she said no.

'What would you like to hear?'

'Count Basie,' I said.

She didn't have anything by him. But she had some Beethoven.

'Ain't you got no good music?' I said after a while.

'Why, this is the best music there is!' she says.

'That may be a fact,' I says, 'but it sure don't do much for me.'

That did it. She got to telling me all about Booker T. Washington and how he was born a slave and how later on in his life he had tea with Queen Victoria. I got to trying to figure out what all this had to do with these violins that was sawing away, then it hit me, right sudden-like, that this woman must think she's Queen Victoria. I said to myself, half-listening to her and half not, 'But if she thinks she's Queen Victoria, I wonder who in the hell she think *I* am?'

You know how it is when a woman gets to talking: Yakkity-Queen Victoria-yak. Yakkity-Booker T. Washington-yak. I sat there listening and nodding. The music stopped then, and she got up to change the record. Still talking.

'Are you a virgin?' I said. She stopped talking then. She turned around and looked at me, her eyes real wide.

'What did you say?'

'I said are you a virgin?'

The faucet in the kitchen was running. She went in and turned it off, and all I could hear was my leather belt creaking each time I took a breath. Then she said, from the kitchen, 'Yes. Yes, I am. But what make you ask that?' Only she didn't say it just like that. She spoke real proper.

'I just wondered,' I said. I got up and took my jacket off, and when she come back in the living-room I was sitting there in my shirtsleeves.

'Well, Mr ——,' she called me by my name, 'I think you better go now.'

'I ain't got a mind to leave right now. In fact, I'd sho appreciate some more tea.'

'No, I think you'd better leave.'

'I done told you once I ain't going no-place. Will you get me some more tea, or do I have to get it myself?'

'I'll get it,' she said. 'But after that I'm afraid you have to leave.'

'We won't think about that right now.'

When she brought the tea I said, 'I think I'll take it over here.' I got up from the chair and went to the couch. She handed the cup to me and I seen that her hand was shaking a little. She took and got her own cup and saucer and sat in the chair.

'What made you ask that?'

'You look it.'

'I look it?'

'Yeah. And *act* it, too.'

'But that's impossible!'

'Nothing's impossible. Come over here and sit by me.'

'No.'

'Do I have to come and get you?'

'But it's . . . it's not quite *true*!?'

'What's not true? Come on over here.'

'You're being impossible.'

'Everybody's impossible. Come here.'

'I absolutely *refuse*!?'

When she was sitting beside me, with about enough room between us for a fair-sized hat box, I said, 'Now tell me 'bout it.'

Real sob story. She'd been engaged to some nigger in Philadelphia all during the war—he was in the army and she'd done waited for him faithful-like—and for three years after the war. They was waiting, she said, till he got out of medical school before they got married. He graduated alright. Got his MD and everything. Then lo and behold the nigger takes off for Europe with a little white gal from the University of Pennsylvania.

I felt sorry for her. I really did. In fact, I felt so sorry for her that the upshot of the matter was we was holding hands, and that hat box woulda had to be *mighty* small to get between us by this time. I asked her what she meant by this 'not quite true' business, but she was vague about that. All she would say was 'the affair was not consumeded', whatever she meant by that.

I think you know how a man feels in a situation like that. You be sitting right close to a nice-looking woman, and she gets to telling you how some man done her wrong. You get to feeling sorry for her. But because she look so *good* you get to feeling strong, too. Then you get to feeling wrong about being strong. Then after a while you don't feel wrong no more. All you feel is *strong*!

'Yeah,' I said. 'That was real tough.'

'It sure was. But life goes on.'

'It sho do. You want to hear some music?'

'I thought you didn't like it.'

'I don't; but since you do we may's well listen to it.'

'Alright.'

I started to winding up the victrola.

'No,' she said, 'let's play the radio instead.'

'The radio?'

'Yes.'

I didn't know she had a radio. She went inside the bed-room and got a small radio and plugged it in in the living-room. When she sat down again I tried to kiss her.

'Don't,' she said.

When I kissed her her lips was real tight. But by the end of the Weekly Summary of the News they won't tight no more.

Afterwards, back at my own place with a decent drink, I got to thinking about it. Now what in God's name make a man act like that? I didn't have no intentions of marrying the woman. In fact, I didn't even want to *see* her more than two or three times the week, and then out of pure selfishness.

'Will you be here tomorrow?' she asked when I was leaving.

'Sho I will.'

'Promise?'

'And hope to die if I don't, honey.'

'You're *such* a nice man. I always *did* like you.'

I didn't say nothing.

'Think you'll love me just a little?'

'You know I will, honey.'

'Alright,' she said. 'Good-bye, darling!'

'Bye-bye, now.'

'Sleep tight!'

'I'll do my best,' I said.

I knowed what would happen, of course: niggers would get to signifying, and I'd get mad. I'd get to ducking Miss Florence, and *she'd* get mad.

I took off my clothes and poured me another drink—a big one—drank it, turned out the lights and got into bed and pulled the covers over my head tight, *real* tight, and went to sleep.

A FINE ROMANCE

It was sitting there chewing on the sandwich and looking out the window that I took any notice of him. You know how it is when you're sitting in a train with somebody on the seat opposite yours: you both look out the window and your two reflections can see each other, it seems like, so that you can look into the other person's eyes through the glass in the window.

I'd gotten on the train in Birmingham, where I'd been to see my father for the weekend. It was him who had made the sandwich and given it to me, because he knows that 'possum is my favourite kind of meat. I didn't pay too much attention to the man when I first sat down, because it ain't my habit to go around looking at strange men. But now, chewing on the sandwich and looking at him through the window, he looked so handsome that it made me kind of twitch inside. 'Mary-Jane Jessup?' I said to myself, 'you's a growed married woman. Don't you go thinking like you was free, single and twenty-one.'

The man looked away from the window right then, and as he did I looked down at my sandwich real quick and took a big bite out of it, just like nothing had happened. I could feel him looking at my face, then at my legs. I knew my lips were a mite greasy from the sandwich, and I wished I'd waited until I got home before I ate it. The man looked away right casual-like and got to fishing in his pocket for something. I looked up from the sandwich and our eyes met for a brief instant. He got what it was from his pocket—it was a Zippo cigarette lighter—and took out the insides of it. I sat there and watched him through the window. He took a tin bottle from another pocket, opened it, and squeezed a few drops of fluid into the cotton filling inside the lighter. Through the window I could see the countryside all red-earthed and scraggly-treed, at the same time I saw him light a cigarette and put the lighter and fluid back in his pockets. Then he looked out the window again—or maybe it was in it—and as we went by a brick building that looked like a schoolhouse I could see his eyes: big and brown and pear-shaped.

There was no expression on his face at all; nary a one. Every once in a while his eyes would flicker, like he seen something go by that interested him; but that was all. 'Shoot,' I said to myself. 'This man ain't even thinking about me. In fact, he might not even be looking into my eyes at all!' So I leaned back and closed my eyes. But every time I opened them I found myself looking dead smack into his. Anyway, I fell asleep. Or almost asleep, it looks to me now.

'How far you going?'

'You speaking to me?'

'Sure I'm speaking to you. Ain't nobody else sitting with us, is it?'

31

'Don't get cute with me, mister,' I said. 'I don't talk to people I ain't been introduced to proper. I'm a lady.'

He laughed. Right cocky laugh he had, too. In spite of myself I wasn't angry.

'How far you going?' he said again.

'I gets off at Talladega.'

'That ain't too long a ways from here.'

'It's long enough.'

'You live in Talladega, or you got kinfolks there?'

'I live in a little town outside it,' I said. And then, looking him dead in them big brown eyes: 'With my husband.'

His expression didn't change any more than a statue's would.

'Been married long?'

'Ten years.'

'Ten years?'

'Uh-huh.'

'You sure don't look it. Look to me like you ain't been married but four years. Five, at the most. You sure you ain't lying?'

'What reason I got to lie to you?'

'Any ten I can think of. You been married that long, sure 'nough?'

'Yes, sir. Ten years this month.'

'Any children?'

'I got two boys, and one of them is grown. But I still don't see what all this got to do with you.'

'Maybe nothing, maybe a lot,' he said. He leaned back and closed his eyes and sighed. 'Ho, ho, ho,' he said. I sat there looking at him and wondering what in the devil he was up to anyway; him and his 'Ho, ho, ho'.

'I'm going on up to Charlotte,' he said after a while.

'Are you?'

'I sure am.'

'What's that got to do with me?'

He didn't say nothing to that. There was a train coming from the other direction. I could just barely hear it whistle, a long way away, like the cry of a great black grandmother calling you home. Then all of a sudden there it was, right on top of us, and as it rushed by it sounded like the pop of a puffed-up paper bag. The man jumped and moved his head in a little, and our eyes met one more time.

'What time we get to Talladega?'

'What time *we* get to Talladega?'

'Alright. What time do the train get to Talladega?'

'I don't rightly know. Around seven o'clock, I reckon. Why?'

'Somebody meeting you?'

I knew there wasn't nobody meeting me, but I remembered right then that I had some washing to do for Mrs Ryan and I was already a day late with it. But she wouldn't mind, would she? Yeah, she might. She might start taking their clothes over to Jane Freeman's. No, she wouldn't do that. I'm the best laundress in town.

'No,' I said. 'Ain't nobody meeting me, but I got to get on home.

'Ain't no such thing as *got* to, is it?'

'Maybe for you there ain't, but there sure is for me.'

'I was thinking of getting off at Talladega and—'

'No.'

'—and catching the next train. And I was wondering if you'd like to have a drink with me.'

'No.'

'How 'bout some coffee?'

'No. I done told you I got to get home.'

'Ain't no harm in just a cup of coffee, is it? After all, you don't live but once. . .'

'I done told you I . . . alright. But just for a cup of coffee.'

We got off the train together at Talladega. Didn't nobody else get off with us, so we walked down the platform together with him carrying both my suitcase in one hand and his in the other. He was good and strong, alright, just like I'd thought. We checked the suitcases in the waiting room and walked down the street to a little place I know called Millers' Bar. We sat in a back booth and he told me all about hisself, where he was born and who reared him and all. But I wasn't listening. I was looking at his eyes: big and brown and pear-shaped.

'You reckon we could—'

'No.'

'Couldn't the train be an hour or two late? Won't nobody check, will they?'

'I done told you five times I got to get home. Besides, you said just for a cup of coffee, didn't you?'

I smiled at him, and he laughed. He had a nice mouth.

Outside in the taxi I could feel his hand on my shoulder, then at the back of my neck. 'God forgive me,' I said as I nestled up to him. 'Please, God, forgive me.'

When I opened my eyes I was looking through the window at three water tanks set on girders high in the air. I knew good and well they were familiar, but somehow I couldn't place them right off. Then I seen what it was that waked me. The door to the railroad car was open, and the rails were making a great racket. Just then the conductor stuck his head through the doorway and said, 'Talladega next! Talladega!' I opened my purse and put on some powder and lipstick and combed my hair. The man was asleep; or leastways his eyes were closed. When I finished making-up I closed my purse and got up and started to taking my bags down from the rack. He opened his eyes, then, and looked up at me and said, 'Can I help you?'

'Thanks a lot,' I said. When he got up I saw that he wasn't as tall as I thought he would be; and his voice was pitched a little higher than I imagined. When the train was in the station he said, 'You go on ahead', and took both my bags and handed them to me one by one on the platform.

'Thanks a whole lot,' I said.

'It was nothing,' he said.

I walked down the platform and then to the bus station and went on home to my husband.

A SOUND OF SCREAMING

I had my jacket slung over my shoulder, and I could feel the lining of it growing hot against my back. I was kind of tired, and I reckoned that the girl was too. We'd walked over five miles. When we got to a good-sized tree I said, 'Let's us sit down.' We moved off the road, and I spread my jacket for her to sit on. She began to cry. I eased her off my jacket a little bit so's I could get to the pocket my cigarettes was in. When I got to the pack I seen there wasn't but one cigarette left. I lit it and handed it to her. She took it, but didn't take a drag on it. She just sat there holding it with one hand and wiping her eyes with the other. As I watched the smoke slide upwards I got to thinking about the time we were in a nightclub in Memphis—we'd gone up there for the weekend to see Erskine Hawkins and his Orchestra—and she was holding a cigarette just as she was now, in that loose way she has so that it looks like she's about to drop it. That was a balling weekend. That was when it happened.

'Miz Turner said it won't hurt much,' I said. Even while I was saying it I knew it wasn't the thing to say; and long after I said it, even after we'd gotten up and started walking again, I could hear it: 'Miz Turner said it won't hurt much.'

The girl didn't say anything. I sat there envying her the cigarette—wishing she'd take a drag on it and hand it to me and trying to think of something pleasant to say. I carried on a conversation with her in my mind.

'You know I love you, don't you, Maybelle?'

'Uh-hunh,' she'd say. 'I know it.'

'You know that if there was any way possible to get out of this I wouldn't let you go through with it, don't you?'

'I know that, James,' she'd say. 'I know that.'

Instead I said, out loud, 'We ain't got much further to go.'

She was still crying. I put my arm around her and drew her to me. 'Hush,' I said, and kissed her on the temple. Her hair was wet and smelled of tears and sweat. 'Hush, now,' I said. 'Ain't no need of acting up like that.' I felt like I was her father.

All of a sudden, in that funny way women have of changing from one mood to the next like their minds operate on invisible strings, she stopped crying. 'Come on, James,' she said. 'We better be getting on.' We got up, and after I'd dusted my jacket off we started down the road.

We were going to a place called Kapalachee. It's so small it ain't even listed on county maps, let alone Alabama or United States of America maps. The first thing you come to on the road we took is a big magnolia tree. Right along-side of it is a white frame house with Greek columns and a little ways down, just after a grocery store with a neon Pepsi-Cola sign, is the coloured section. When we got to the magnolia tree I said, 'You want to rest a while?'

'We almost there, ain't we?'

'Yeah,' I said.

'Then come on.'

The girl won't but nineteen, but I felt right then like I was her son.

I had a picture in my mind of the house we were going to. It belongs to a woman named Miz Thomas. Miz Turner had told us it was the biggest house in that part of town. I figured there'd be a big living-room with lots of nice furniture and bare floors. I figured there'd be a sign, a nice one with fringes, saying 'Home Sweet Home' or 'God Bless Our Home'.

I was right about everything except the floors. There was a big rug in the living-room, and so many small cloth ones that I kept tripping over them. There were lots of little doodars around, too, on the mantelpiece and on the tables: glass elephants and giraffes and ostriches and things, and on the centre table a group of three monkeys, the kind you see everywhere: Hear nothing, See nothing, Say nothing.

I was wrong, too, about Miz Thomas. I'd always imagined that women who do that kind of work would be big and fat and evil-looking. But Miz Thomas wasn't big, she wasn't fat, and she wasn't evil-looking. She was a woman in her late thirties, I'd say, kind of thin, with a pleasant face. In fact, she looked just like the kind of person you'd expect to see pushing somebody's baby down the street on a Sunday afternoon. When we told her that Miz Turner'd sent us she acted like we were old friends. After we'd chit-chatted a while she said, 'Well, I reckon we'd best get started.'

I stood up and paid her what Miz Turner had told me to, and after she'd counted the money she and the girl got up. 'You can stay out here if you want to,' she said, 'or you take a walk. Either way is OK with me.'

'Thanks,' I said, 'I think I'll take a walk.'

'Alrighty. We'll see you in about half an hour.'

'A half-hour?'

'Mmmm . . . make it forty-five minutes.'

I left. I'd wanted to say something to the girl, but what was I going to say? 'Good luck'? The damn thing about life is, it seemed to me then, that there ain't never anything to say when life and death is involved. So I just left.

I walked down the street, trying my best not to think of anything. But it didn't work. I found myself picturing what was going on back there at Miz Thomas's. Then, walking by a bunch of children playing, I could hear the girl screaming. I walked away and tried to think of something else, but that didn't work, either. I could still hear the poor child screaming, screaming with pain, and Miz Thomas saying, 'Hush, now! It won't be long!'

I went into a store and bought me a bottle of wine. I could still hear the sound of screaming, and it was nearbout driving me crazy. I felt like ripping the top off the bottle and drinking the wine right there. I walked out the store and looked around for a shady tree, and when I found one I set down under it and opened the bottle. The wine was sweet, and the gurgling sound it made when I drank drowned out the screaming some. I thought of saying a prayer for the girl, but I figured it would be disreligious to pray while I was drinking, so I didn't. I got to wondering what the child would have been, a boy or a girl, and who it would have looked like most, the girl or me. After about the third swig of wine I got to wondering whether it would have been a boy or girl at all. 'God forgive me,' I said out loud, and took a good long swig.

I got to thinking about women: about the two of them standing there in the living-room, the girl and Miz Thomas. I don't reckon I'll ever forget the way the girl looked, standing there waiting: just waiting, with nary an expression on her face, like a passenger on a train. And Miz Thomas with that look of half-greediness and half-wisdom on her face, like she knew something secret but would drain the very life out of you before she told it. I got to thinking about the fact that women never seem to talk about anything important; leastways when I'm around. It's always spring hats, last year's boy friend, going to church, coming from church . . . anything but about being a woman. Men can set down and talk for hours about everything under the sun; but not women. I reckon the thing is that they give life, and one thing about life is that it don't never talk about itself: it just is. Leastways that was what I was thinking, drinking my wine.

When I got up I was half-drunk and full-unhappy. I walked back to Miz Thomas's house and rang the doorbell. There was no answer. I rang it again and waited. No answer. What a nice front porch, I thought. A real nice house. If it won't for them monkeys me and the girl could live here real nice. It would have been a girl, too, I bet. Ugly and wrinkled at first, like most babies, then pretty once she come out the hospital. Still no answer. I rang the bell again, long and hard. Miz Thomas came to the door.

'Hi,' she said. Smiling.

'How is she?'

She looked at me like I'd asked something outrageous. 'She's fine!' she said.

Can I see her?'

'Sure. Come on in. She's in that room right over there.' She pointed.

When I got into the room the girl was lying on the bed fully undressed. I thought she'd look tired and exhausted, but she didn't. If you'd seen her face you'd have sworn she'd just come from a party. I didn't feel surprised or relieved or sad or happy or nothing. I just stood there leaning against the door and looking at her. She never looked prettier, I swear; nice brown skin like underdone toast, black hair falling around her shoulders. I went over and kissed her and hated myself for wanting her.

'How'd it go? Did it hurt much?'

'It wasn't bad.'

'That's fine,' I said. 'That's just fine.'

'Where'd you go?'

'I took a walk.'

'I know, but where?'

'Just around. How you feel, Maybelle?'

'I feel fine.'

'Can you walk?'

'Sure I can walk!'

'Then let's get out of here.'

'I can't, right now.'

'How come you can't?'

'Miz Thomas said I got to lay down a half-hour.'

'Then will you be alright?'

'I don't know.'

'What you mean you don't know?'

'It ain't over yet.'

'Ain't *over* yet . . .'

'No. It takes . . . don't let's talk about it, James Jessup. Please don't let's talk about it. Tell me where 'bouts you been.'

'Just around, Maybelle. I done told you I just walked around. How come it ain't over yet?'

'Tell me what you seen, James Jessup,' she said. She pulled my head down and my face was in the pillow beside her and I could hear her hair like thunder in my ears. 'Tell me everything.'

'I saw an old white man,' I said, talking into the pillow and not thinking of what I was saying but just talking, 'in a brown overcoat. It seemed kind of strange because I'd never seen anybody wear an overcoat in the summer before. I saw a bow-legged boy rolling a hoop down the street with a stick, and just before he got to me the hoop wavered and fell like a coin when it stops spinning. I saw a cloud in the sky that looked like a horse and then I saw roses and people and houses and when I looked at the cloud again it didn't look like a horse, it looked like a woman with wild hair. I set down under a tree and there was a huge heart carved on the bark of it with an arrow through it and the initials V.H. and A.R. How you feeling, Maybelle?'

'Tell me some more.'

'How come it ain't over yet?'

'It takes twenty-four hours. Tell me some more, James.'

'Twenty-four *hours*! . . .'

'Yes.'

'Jesus Christ,' I said. I raised up from the pillow.

'You ought not to say that,' the girl said. 'You done told me plenty times not to say that.'

'Hush,' I said.

'Don't tell me to hush. You the Deacon of the church, ain't you? You ought to . . .'

'Hush!'

'You ought to know better than that. And a married man to boot. You really should know a heap better, James Jessup. You with a grown son almost my age. You old enough to be my daddy, James? Tell me. You know everything, don't you? Then why don't you answer me that? Huh? Ain't you got nothing to say? You that's got the message of God and gives it to the people each and every Sunday?' She grunted, and laughed. 'You gave me a message, alright. Yes, sir. I got *your* message.'

I didn't say anything. I was lying flat on my back now, staring up at the ceiling with the girl young and naked and brown beside me. When she'd calmed down I said, 'Do we have to stay here all that time?'

'No, we can go in a while. It happens tomorrow.'

'Miz Thomas going be there?'

'No. She's done all she got to do.'

'You sure?'

'Sure I'm sure. What time is it?'

'Four-thirty.'

'I got seven more minutes to lay here.' She crossed her legs and sighed. I hated myself all over again for wanting her so bad.

•

There was one bus from Kapalachee to where we lived that left at six-thirty every evening, and we took it. Nothing happened on the way. We sat on the back seat and the girl slept with her head on my shoulder most of the way. When we got close to home I started thinking of people we might meet, and what they'd think and say. The girl must have been thinking the same thing because she said, just before the bus stopped, 'I reckon I'd best go on home alone.' I didn't say anything because it wasn't the time to argue. When we got off the bus I took her by the arm and started towards my place.

'James, I reckon I'd better go on home.'

'I'm taking you over to my place.'

'You know what people will say, James: "His wife ain't been gone a month and him running around with that girl. And him the Deacon of . . ."'

'Hush,' I said. 'Each and every one of us got his own life to live. If you start worrying about what people think and say you'll wind up in a corner with an umbrella over your head. Come on.'

'My daddy'll kill you if he ever find out.'

'I ain't studying 'bout your daddy. I'm not only older than him but bigger, too.'

When we got to my place I pulled the blinds and turned the lights on. The girl sat on the bed. I took my jacket off and went to the cupboard to see how much liquor there was, because I figured the girl might need it. There was almost a full bottle of Old Mr Boston, and I was happy. I poured a drink in a shot glass and handed it to her. Then I poured myself a drink and said 'Here's to it,' but she'd already drank hers.

'Miz Thomas said I was to walk around a lot.'

'Walk? How come?'

'She says that makes it easier.'

I thought for a while—in spite of what I told her I really didn't relish the idea of anybody seeing us together—then I said, 'How about dancing, then?'

'Yeah!' she said.

We must have danced for over an hour: me guiding her and she following, close and warm, with all the sins in the whole wide world spinning round and round in my brain.

'Wait a minute,' she said. We stopped dancing.

'What's the matter?'

'Nothing. Wait a minute.' She put a hand to her forehead and sat on the bed. I sat down beside her and moved her hand away and put my own where hers had been. Her forehead was warm, but I couldn't tell whether she had a fever or not. She put a hand to her stomach and made a face. Not a real painful face, but the kind a woman makes whenever she sees something she don't like.

'I reckon I'd better call Dr Hall.'

'Don't be no fool, James.'

'Does it hurt real bad?'

'Nnn-nnn.'

'After you've rested a while I think we ought to dance some more.'

'I don't feel like it.'

'It'll make it easier for you. Miz Thomas must know what she's talking about so you ought to—'

'I done told you I don't feel like it. Leave me alone, James. Please leave me alone.'

45

She lay down and turned over on her right side, facing me, with her hand resting on her stomach. I got up and started to look around for a coverlet or blanket to throw over her, but changed my mind. She was sweating. I changed the record on the machine and put on 'Second Balcony Jump' by Earl Hines. I turned it up loud.

'Come on,' I said. 'Let's jump to Father Hines.' I took her by the hand and began pulling her up from the bed.

'Don't, James.'

'Come on.'

'No, don't.'

'Let's get with it, Sugar. That's Little Benny Harris on the trumpet. Little Benny's your favourite, isn't he?' I snapped my fingers m time to the music with one hand and pulled her up with the other. She sort of half-laughed and half-cried and got up. I held her close, and we moved around in a two-step offtime. When the trumpet solo started I riffed along with it into her ear.

Tee-deet tee-deet tah-dah,
Teeeet-tee dee-dee-deet . . .

'Feel better?'

'Uh-hunh. A little.'

I kissed her cheek and held her closer. After a while I could feel her fingernails in my back, and just for a brief instant I could hear the screaming again, like I did back in Kapalachee. I moved back a little.

When the record was over I didn't put on another one, but poured two drinks and handed her the bigger one. She drank it as if it was medicine and lay back on the bed. She looked good, lying there. Looking down at her I thought, 'What the hell, that would be better than walking or dancing, wouldn't it?' and called myself the dirtiest name I could think of. Out loud I said, 'I think it's about time you be getting some sleep.'

It must have been about five o'clock in the morning when I woke up. The sun was just rising, and through the blinds the soft light made the room look like rooms look in dreams. The girl's stockings were lying across the arm of a wicker-back chair by the window. Looking at them I imagined, for a moment, that we were back in the hotel room in Memphis. When we got up we'd go to the same restaurant we went to the day before and have a great big bowl of kidney beans and rice. Then maybe we'd go to a movie and see a cartoon and the Warner Brothers News with that camera turning to look you right dead in the eyes: THE END. Later on we'd go to a nightclub, the one where that woman sings almost as good as Sister Rosetta Tharpe. We'd get high and have us an A-grade ball, with her holding her cigarette as if she was about to drop it.

I raised myself up on one elbow and looked at her. I wanted to kiss her, but I was afraid it would wake her. She woke up anyway: moaning. I could see from the way the sheet fell over her that she had her hand to her stomach again; only this time it was lower than it had been the night before. She sighed, and her breath smelled like morning.

'How's it going, Maybelle?'

'Not so hot.'

'Not too hot?'

'Not so hot.'

'Can I get you something?'

'Nnn-nnn.'

'A glass of milk?'

'Nnn-nnn.'

'An orange?'

'No.'

'Can I do anything at all for you?'

'Yeah, you can do something for me. Take me to Chicago. Right now. Chicago, San Francisco, Los Angeles, any place. But now. Right now.' She doubled up right suddenlike, with her knees close to her breasts. Her hair moving against the pillow made a sound like a whist broom when clothes are being brushed. She was crying. I wished right then that I could go through what she was going through: that I could do it for her, or if not for her then with her. But I didn't say it. A man can't say a thing like that to a woman and sound like anything but a damn fool, I thought. So I just lay there with an arm around her, staring up at the ceiling. A short time later she relaxed and laid her head on my chest.

'Tell me something funny,' she said.

'Like what?'

'Like anything. But make it funny.'

'Alright,' I said. 'I'll tell you about *Sam the Man*.' I couldn't remember the story word for word, but I did my best:

Ever hear the tale of Sam?
Sam the Man from Birmingham?

He was a killer from way back.
He'd fall into town sharper'n a tack
With a brand new suit laid on his back;
A pair of blue-black shoes so shine
They looked like elderberry wine.

He'd shake a pair of dice and say,
'Which one of you kiddies wants to play?'
All the kats would gather round
And dice would roll across the ground.
They'd play from morning, noon, 'til night,

Then Sam would run clean out of sight.
They'd search high and they'd cuss low,
But they wouldn't see nothing of Sam no mo'.
He'd grabbed up all the loot and dusted
So fast Jesse Owens would be disgusted.

When I got to 'dusted' the girl laughed and started beating on my chest. Only she wasn't really laughing, I found out. She was making the kind of sound a child makes sometimes, so that you have to wait for a while before you can tell whether it's laughing or crying. So I didn't finish *Sam the Man*. I just lay there and let her beat on my chest a while, and when it got too rough on me I took ahold of her hands.

We laid there for an hour or two, with her tossing and turning and telling me it wasn't any need to get Dr Hall because there was nothing he could do noways. Then I got up and fixed breakfast. I figured she'd want to have it in bed, but she said no. She got up and put some clothes on and sat down to the table. She ate hearty, and I was glad. She didn't have her hand to her stomach any more. In fact, if you'd seen us right then you'd have thought there was nothing at all the matter.

After breakfast she took her clothes off and got back into bed. I tried to get her to dance, or leastways to walk around the room a little, but she wouldn't hear it. In a little while she fell asleep.

I got to cleaning up the place, but I was afraid it would wake her so I stopped. I sat in a chair for a while, but I couldn't stand doing nothing so I got up and started to cleaning up again, real soft-like. When the place was clean I washed the dishes and sat back down. The girl groaned and I looked at her but she was still asleep. I got up and took my shoes out and shined them. I put them under the bed and sat down again. Then I took them out once more and shined them till I could nearbout see the face of God. I went over to the window and looked through the curtains. There was nothing to see but the house across the street, and I'd already seen it eight million times. It needed a fresh coat of paint; *had* needed it for going on two years now. I felt like going out there and painting it. I'd paint the front porch first, just like the front of your body is the first thing you wash, then I'd get the sides and the back. I'd fix the back stairs up where those two steps are loose, then I'd paint them too. Maybe I'd even weed the garden out in back and plant some collard greens and turnips and stuff. I was busy planting when the girl woke up.

'James?'

'Huh?'

'I thought you was gone. What time is it?'

'Nearbout three o'clock. You want something to eat?'

'I ain't hungry.'

'How you feel?'

I don't know. I don't feel nothing at all. Nothing.' She was quiet a while and then she said, 'I been having the craziest dream. You hear me laughing?'

'No.'

'I dreamt I was in a boat with a man. A sailboat; but I couldn't tell whether the man was you or somebody else. Anyway there we was and the man was rowing and telling me a joke. I can't remember what it was now, but it was so funny that we both got to laughing and the boat turned over and there we was in the water, just laughing our fool heads off. You didn't hear me laughing, James?'

'No I didn't, Maybelle.'

'That's when I woke up and felt for you and you wasn't there. You ain't going no-place are you, James?'

'I ain't going no-place, honey.'

'If you do will you take me along with you?'

'Sure I will.'

'What time is it, James?'

'A little after three.'

'A little after what?'

'After three. Don't you want an apple or something?'

'I wish it was after three tomorrow. Or next week.'

'Don't you want an apple?'

'No. You're not going leave, are you, James?'

'You know I wouldn't do that, Maybelle.'

'You sure?'

'You know I wouldn't do nothing like that.'

'Then what you standing so far away for?'

I went over to the bed and sat beside her. Then I leaned over and took her in my arms. 'James,' she said. 'James, James, James.' She was crying, with her fingernails biting into my back.

Around five o'clock I was sitting in a chair reading a funny paper. The girl wasn't crying or groaning or anything, and she wasn't asleep. She got up, real casual-like, and went to the bathroom. She was gone about twenty minutes, I reckon, before she came out, still fully undressed, and turned the record player on. When the record started she got to dancing by herself; not wild or anything, just dancing. I thought that was a good thing, because of what Miz Thomas had said, so I just sat there and watched her: moving her hips and snapping her fingers and looking so fine I could have worshipped her.

'You feel alright?'

'Sure I feel alright,' she said. 'I feel fine.'

'Ain't it about time?'

'Yeah.'

'You reckon Dr Hall might—'

'Ain't no need of no doctor. It's over.'

'*Over . . .*'

'Yeah.'

'Jesus Christ,' I said.

'I told you not to say that,' she said, and laughed. She turned the volume of the record player up, still laughing, and got to dancing right wild-like, kicking her legs around and saying 'Hey, now! *Yeah!*' in time to the music. When she was tired she lay on the bed and looked at me. She smiled. I got up and took the record off, then sat down beside her. She was breathing fast. 'I'm glad it's over,' I said, and leaned over and kissed her. I could see the tiny brown folds in the pupils of her eyes. I kissed her again, soft.

'James,' she said. 'James, don't. Oh, James, darling, please . . . *please* don't. Oh, James,' she said, with her nails biting into my back.

BIG BOY

Even the crows seemed to sense something was up. The first one we seen flew straight down Davis Street, so low you could almost touch it. The few of us that seen it looked at one another, but didn't nobody say a mumbling word. 'Long about three o'clock the next afternoon there was another one, way up high and black 'gainst the blue sky.

It was a heap like that heavy feeling you gets in a town just before a tornado hits it. Won't nobody stirring much, and those of us that was won't paying one another too much of a never-mind. A few of us knew what the matter was, though, because we seen him getting off the train: Big Boy was back in town.

I won't tell you what his real name was, because I'm scared that evil individual will come back and shorten my days on God's green earth; but I'll tell you how he come by his nickname.

It happened like this. He first come to town in July of 1941. At first didn't none of us know where he come from or how long he planned to stay or nothing. We soon found out this much though: he came from East Saint Louis,

Illinois, and every living soul in the United States of America knows that the peoples from East Saint Louis, Illinois, is about the baddest in the country.

He won't no big person, neither, what I mean. About five foot seven he was, and if he weighed more'n a hundred and twenty pounds Abraham Lincoln was a full-blooded Indian. But I'm here to tell you that 'longside of that little nigger a rattlesnake would look like a blessed angel. He had small, squinch eyes and the complexium of black sandpaper what's done been used. That boy looked so evil that every time your eyes met his you felt like getting down on your bended knees and saying 'Gracious Father who are in Heaven, have mercy on ALL mankind'. I mean he was a *bad* member of humanity.

He hadn't been in town two weeks, that first time, before he'd done caused a heap of trouble. He took to coming by the barbershop every evening 'long about five, always dressed sharper'n Dick's hatband in a brown wide-striped suit with a long, double-breasted jacket and the trousers pegged from twenty-five inches at the knees to fourteen at the cuffs. He sported a wide-brimmed felt hat and a gold chain and a pair of knob-toed shoes—the kind that turn up at the toes. We'd all be sitting around telling lies and carrying on and all of a sudden there he'd be, and wouldn't nobody have seen him come in. He was that kind of individual.

One evening we was all sitting around the shop as usual—won't nobody getting a haircut—and I was telling a lie.

'Whyn't you hush, James Turner?' Old Man Maypeck said. 'You done told that same lie eighteen thousand times.'

'You know one we ain't heard, I reckon,' I said. Old Man Maypeck igged me something terrible and turned to Blue Juice. 'Go 'head, Blue Juice,' he said. 'Tell us one.'

We was all crazy about Blue Juice, because he told the damndest lies you ever heard tell of. So Blue Juice got to telling this lie—something about a mosquito the same size and colour as a humming-bird, if I don't disremember—and halfway through it we heard a voice; a real authorizing voice, saying, 'Quit it.'

We all turned around, and there he was: Big Boy.

'Sheeeit,' Blue Juice said. There won't a one of us worried or nothing, least of all Blue Juice, because he was way the bigger of the two. So Blue Juice went on with the lie. Big Boy started down the barbershop.

'Did you hear what I said, my man? I said quit it,' he said, smiling.

'What the hell kind of individual is *you*, man?' Blue Juice said.

'That ain't none of your worryings,' Big Boy said. 'When I say quit it just quit it, that's all.'

'Sheeeit,' Blue Juice said. 'You better gawn, nigger, 'fore you gits hurt.'

'Did you hear what I said, my man?'

'Aw, nigger, you—' Blue Juice started to say, but he never finished. Big Boy had his razor out and *rip, rip, rip!* Blue Juice fell and niggers was scrambling out the back door. And there was Big Boy backing towards the front door with his razor at the ready, chewing gum and grinning like a brass monkey. When he was gone and we'd done fixed Blue Juice up the best we could Old Man

Maypeck said, 'That there's a little nigger, but that there razor he got sure makes him a BIG nigger.'

From then on we called him Big Boy.

For them first three or four days, that second time Big Boy come to town, didn't nothing much happen. Looked like the war had done changed him or something, because from the way he carried hisself it didn't look like he was up to his old transactions. He got talkative even. He didn't come by the barbershop, but took to going to a little café on Robert E. Lee Street called 'The Bee Hive'. He'd come in 'long about nine with his eyes real shine like he'd been smoking weed and say, 'I'm Mr Riddick from Chappaquidick. I'm so hip I can't quit it.' Looked like he liked that, because he'd say it over and over and each time he'd take a drink of moonshine out of one o' them paper cups they sell coke in. Looked like he learned a whole lot during the war. He even knowed 'The Signifying Monkey', and he'd stand there by the jukebox and rattle it off in that high-pitched, faggity voice he had:

> Said the monkey to the lion
> In the woods one day,
> 'There's a BAD motherhubber
> Down the road a way.'

He'd say the whole thing from beginning to end, rattling it off faster'n a tobacco salesman. But wouldn't nobody have nothing to do with him.

For a while it looked like nothing would happen at all. Blue Juice was in town and he'd done swore he'd get his revengance; but he'd seen Big Boy three or four times, and each time they'd greeted one another like old friends.

'How you doing, Big Boy?'

'Mighty fine, my man, how's yourself?

'Just fine, thanks.'

And they'd walk on. We all got to breathing easier.

One fine day a whole bunch of us was standing outside the barbershop shooting the breeze. A pretty woman walked by and we all got to signifying at her. After she was gone went inside and sat down.

'Well,' Blue Juice said, 'I reckon I'll get me a haircut.'

We all laughed, even though we'd heard Blue Juice say that a thousand times. He had a head like a watermelon, with just about that much hair on it. His face had so many scars on it that it looked like a railroad junction. He sat down in one of the chairs and the barber-man covered him with that white cloth they all have and lathered his face so's he could give him a shave.

And all of a sudden there was Big Boy, smiling.

The place got so quiet that if molasses had've been flowing it would've sounded like a waterfall. Two or three peoples remembered all-of-a-sudden-like that they had business to tend to, and. left right smartly. Blue Juice was leaned way back in the barber-chair with his face all lathered up and his eyes closed. Big Boy stood there in the doorway twirling his gold chain and smiling. Then—you know the way barbers do, they click their scissors at nothing but clean, fresh air before they gets to your headhair—the scissors got to clicking at the chair next to Blue Juice's. The barber-man got to shaving Blue Juice, and you could hear the razor scraping 'most loud as a board against dry cement. All this time Big Boy just stood there, smiling and twirling his gold chain. When the barber-man was through with Blue Juice old Watermelon-head raised hisself up and took the white cloth off of him. He stood up in front of the mirror and felt his chin. Then he seen Big Boy.

He smiled. They stood there, both of them, smiling at one another through the mirror. After a while Blue Juice said, 'Well I'll be a monkey's little sister. Look who's here. How you doing, Big One?'

'Ain't no flies on me,' Big Boy said. 'How 'bout y'self?'

'Aw . . . I'll live, I reckon.'

'Sure glad to hear it.'

'How much I owe you, my man?' Blue Juice said to the barber-man.

'That'll be seventy-five cents,' the barber-man said.

I forgot to tell you all that Big Boy had done changed his way of dressing. Looked like while he was overseas during the war he'd taken to fancier clothes, because he'd taken to wearing pretty red silk shirts. I happen to remember it because didn't any of us see him drop his chain and reach for his razor, he was that fast; just there it was, looking evil and pretty and shiny against the red shirt.

Looking back on it, though, I figure he must have taken it out when Blue Juice reached into his back pocket for the money to pay the barber-man; or rather *made* like that was what he was doing. But Big Boy was right. Blue Juice had his razor out.

Peoples scrambled out the back door so fast you'd have thought they seen a haint. SHOOM! . . . and won't nobody there but me, Old Man Maypeck, and the two of them. They was standing there with their razors at the ready, just out of reach of one another, tense as two tom cats. Smiling.

'Do something, James Turner,' Old Man Maypeck said. 'Don't stand there trembling like a newborn pup. *Do* some thing!'

'Y'all ought not do that,' I said.

'Hush,' Blue Juice said.

They'd started to circling one another, the two of them, feinting at one another and moving their feet like boxers. 'Aaaap!' Big Boy would say when Blue Juice feinted at him. 'Aaaap!' Smiling his brass-toothed smile. When the fight started for real they kept up one of the friendliest conversations I've heard in my natural life.

'How's things in East Saint Louis, Big One?' *Rip!*

'Things is swinging.' *Rip, rip!*

'That's enough, y'all,' Old Man Maypeck said. 'Quit it!'

'Tend to your business, old man,' Big Boy said. 'How's your mother, Blue Juice, is she alright?' *Rip!*

'She's just as healthy as ever, thanks.' *Rip, rip, rip!*

They stopped, then, just like somebody had done given them some kind of signal.

'Well, I reckon we might as well finish it,' Big Boy said.

'Yeah, I reckon we might as well,' Blue Juice said. Then they stood in the middle of the floor and sliced one another they to absolute bits. Smiling.

Big Boy fell first. He just dropped his arms and sagged down like a sack of salt. Blue Juice leaned hisself up against the perfume counter, just in front of the second chair. About this time the peoples—they'd been watching all the time through the back door screen—started to coming back into the barbershop.

'You alright, Blue Juice?'

'Somebody get Dr Hall.'

'Ain't no need of no doctor. That there's a dead nigger.'

'I ain't studying Big Boy. Get a doctor for Blue Juice.'

Blue Juice fell then. Smiling.

When the police come they just took one look at the two of them laying there on the floor, with nary an expression on their faces, then they got back into their car and drove off. After a while an ambulance come up and took them away.

Then we all went home.

SUZIE Q.

Looks like I knowed it from the jump, like I could see the whole story when I first looked at her and there wasn't a thing I could do about it. That ever happen to you? You ever find yourself in a great big hassle and say to yourself, 'This was just what I *thought* would happen.' You know what I'm talking about? Listen to this one:

I'd been eating in this restaurant for going on two years, same time every day of God's week. Goes in and takes off my jacket and washes my hands at one o' them little spigot-taps they got up side the wall and sets down. Didn't even have to order no more. They'd see me coming and start to fixing up this and that, and by the time I set down there it was. A man likes that, you know what I mean?

Now, I'm a man that keeps to myself. I ain't the kind of individual that gets to jawing 'bout the entire political history of America every time he sees a stranger. I knowed most of the people that ate in this place from the face, but if you was to come up to me and say, 'You know so 'n so?' I'd have to say 'No', even though I been copping a scarf right side of him since Pluto was a pup. So when this

62

woman comes up to me this day and says, 'You know James Turner?' I turned around and looked at her.

'No,' I says, 'I don't recollect the pleasure of having met the gentleman.' I runs my eyes over her right quick one time, and it look to me right then that whoever this Turner individual was he had himself aholt to something *fine*.

'You comes in here of-ten?' she says.

'Yeah,' I says. 'Each and every day saving Sundays.'

I seen the whole thing right then, Huss, I swear I did. Something say to me, 'Pee-Wee? You know what you doing? Watch it, Huss! *Watch* it!' But like a fool I didn't pay the voice no never-mind, and instead of turning around and tending to my own business I keeps looking at her.

'Tall, freckle-face fella.'

'Tall, freckle-face fella?'

'Uh-huh.'

Yeah, I said to myself. I know that nigger. Got a head like a turnip. Works in a brickyard.

'Naw,' I says, 'I don't recollect the pleasure of having met the gentleman. But if anybody of that prescription come in I'll be happy to oblige . . .'

'That's mighty kind of you,' she says. 'My name is Suzie Q. Tell 'im I'm looking for him.'

'I sure will do that,' I says. 'I certainly will do that, Miss Suzie,' and kind of raises up off the stool and touches my cap.

'Thanks,' she says, and walks out the door. And as she walked out that door, Pops, my little heart walked right out with 'er. That woman won't built, Daddy, she was con-*struc*ted. One o' them soft, heavy kind that weigh 'bout one three five, about five foot seven of pure heaven. One o' them mellow browns with long eyelashes that get to batting when they talk. One o' them kind of women that make every living creature over the age of FIVE turn they head when she walk by. So lemme tell you.

That afternoon I goes back to my hustle. But there won't much working I could do, Huss, 'cause that big fine body was on my mind. Look like every time I try to lift something I just couldn't *make* it, man, you know what I mean? So I goes up to the boss man and I says, 'Look-a-here, Boss, ain't much I can be doing this evening because I don't feel right.'

'Warl,' he says—you know how white peoples talk— 'Warl, I reckorn you can take the rest of the afternoon orf, Peer-Weer.'

So I takes off. It was one o' them lazy afternoons with the trees waving and carrying on up there in the sky and niggers and white folks going about they transactions in a casual fashion. Like I said from the jump, it looked to me like I knowed everything that was going to happen, so when I sees Suzie Q. tipping down the street the least surprised party was me, y'understand? I looked away and acted right casual, 'cause I know from experience that the best way to lose a woman is let her know you's interested. Womens like *friend*ship. A lot of men don't know that. So when she gets abreast to me I turns away like I don't recognize her.

'Hi!' she says. 'Ain't you the one? . . .'

'Beg pardon?'

'Ain't you the one I was talking to in the restaurant?'

'Oh!' I says. 'Oh, yeah. You find 'im?'

'No,' she says. 'God knows *where* that nigger is?'

'Uh-huh,' I says. 'That's too bad. But if I can be of some service to you I'd sure be delightful.'

'That's right kind of you,' she says, 'but I don't believe there's nothing you can do.'

'Uh-huh,' I says. 'I don't mean to be precurious or nothing like that but what's the trouble?'

'It ain't a matter of being precurious,' she says, and bats them pretty lashes at me. 'It's just that . . .'

'You going some place in a hurry?'

'It's just that today is my day off and that's the onliest time I gets to see him, and that no-good nigger ain't even around!'

'Uh-huh,' I says. 'You going some place in a hurry?'

She looked kind of undecided so I said right quick, 'I don't mean to be butting in or nothing like that but it look to me like you and me's in the same boat. I got a day off today myself with nothing but time on my hands and I thought maybe you and me could . . .'

'Oh, I couldn't do nothing like *that*,' she says. 'What kind of girl you think I am!'

I don't think you get what I mean. I seldom gets a day off myself, so I know how it is. I was thinking maybe you and me could take us a walk some place or go to a picture show or something. But it would be *inner*cent, you see what I'm talking 'bout?'

Well . . .' she says. 'I don't know.'

'We could walk down to the river and watch the boats go by or maybe we could take us a walk out to Kapalachee. But would be *inner*cent, you see what I mean?'

'Well . . . Long as it's *inner*cent.'

'You can trust me, Miss Suzie,' I said, and taken aholt of her arm. When I touched her she was so soft I felt like hollering right *loud* one time, but like I said you's got to be cool with womenfolks. So I litted me up a *cee*gar and we walks up the block.

I told her my name and told her where I work and how long I been working there so that she could see I was a nice, respectable person. I told her about my room (mentioned it right casual-like) and told her I live by myself and done my own cooking and stuff. That's the way you got to work with women. You got to get they sympathy. So then I left her in one of them little cafés near where I live and went upstairs and washed myself real good. And do you know, Jack, that all the time I knowed things won't going turn out right? You think I'm bulling you? I knowed it, man! But I was thinking about that *body,* Jack, I wasn't studying that little voice that kept saying to me, 'Pee-Wee? Watch it, now! *Watch* it!' I gets dressed and hits the road back to the café.

'Nice day, ain't it?'

'It's one o' the prettiest days I seen in my natural life,' I says. 'You been around these parts before?'

'I come up from Biloxi,' she says. 'There peoples I work with come up here so I come up with them.'

'Uh-huh,' I says. We walks along slow-like. 'You like it around here?'

'I kind of miss my kinfolks,' she says. 'James Turner is the first person I met here and I ain't seen him for a week.'

'Uh-huh,' I says. She talked that real soft woman talk that gets in your blood and keeps you awake at nights.

'What you want to do?' I says. 'You want to go to a picture show, or you want to take a walk?'

'What's on at the show?

'A shoot-em-up,' I says. Then I caught myself and said, 'I mean a Westren.'

'A Westren?'

'Yeah. You like Westrens? They got a double-future on today.'

'I don't mind,' she says.

'OK,' I says. 'Let's go.'

We set way up in the back row of the balcony, way away from the bulk of niggers that was carrying on like they didn't have good home-training.

Before I go on let me ask you something. You ever set beside a pretty woman and every time she cross her legs you can hear a rustling and scrustling 'neath her clothes? Well if you have then you know what I'm talking about. Because I'm here to tell you, Lover, that between the white peoples shooting themselves up on the screen and the niggers raising hell in the balcony and Suzie Q. rustling and scrustling every time she cross them big fine legs I didn't think I'd *make* it, Huss! I mean, a man can stand just so much, y'understand? There's a limit to *every*-thing, you dig what I'm talking 'bout? And to make matters worser, one time Miss Q. crossed them legs and her thigh hit up against mine and I didn't know whether to peep or go blind. I was already exaggerated when I got *in* the damn place, y'understand? But by the grace of the almighty God and my own strength of will I stayed cool. Uh-huh, I says to myself. Pee-Wee, you done gone and got yourself some *home*-work.

Hmph-ha. Ha, ha, ha, ha, ha! I didn't know, man! But lemme tell you.

After the show we goes on outside. 'Look-a-here,' I says, 'I don't mean to be personal or nothing like that, but if you wants to come up to my place for a while . . .'

'*Nnnn*-nnh!' she says. 'You done got me wrong, mister. Ain't going be no days like *that*. If that's the kind of woman you wants you better go look someplace else. I'll be seeing you.'

And walks away. I followed her, but not too fast. When I was abreast of her I says, 'Look-a-here,' I says. 'Look-a-here, Miss Suzie, *you's* the one that done *got me* wrong. I ain't like the rest of these niggers round here that will diddle anything from a rattlesnake to a bear—I'm a decent, hard-working man, Miss Suzie, and I'se fully aware that you's got a previous predicament with this here Mr James Turner, so far be it from me to make a intercession between you and him or nothing like that, y'understand what I mean? So don't take no offence to what I said because it was *inner*cent you see what I mean?'

'*Well* . . .' she says, and bats them pretty eyelashes, 'I reckon it's alright. But only for a *little* while.'

So we goes on up to my place.

I'll skip the preliminaries for you, Love. *You* know how main bouts are. First of all the contracts got to be signed and the weights and heights and waist measurements and chest measurements got to be published in the local papers, the national papers, the foreign papers and God only knows where else, then when all the little fights is over—on the night of the main fight—the heavyweights gets into the ring.

The main event started at nine-thirty. I opened up with an uppercut and missed. I followed up with a right and a left and two fast rights and when her defences was down I feinted and jabbed, feinted and jabbed, feinted and feinted and feinted and jabbed until wow! man . . . by the time the bell rang ending the first round I was all set to retire to my corner and cool it for three minutes, but before you could say Sugar Ray Robinson ting-bing! the second round had done started. I'm here to tell you, Lover, that that woman could *fight*.

And man, that was the beginning of the end. The first thing I lost was my job. Suzie Q. would get to showing up at my workplace at odd hours like, say, three-thirty or four in the afternoon. She'd left something at my place, she'd say: a fan or a pair of earrings or a sewing kit . . . just anything or everything. I'd say, 'Here's the key, Sugar. Gawn'n and get it.' She'd say: 'Can't you come with me?' and get to batting them pretty eyelashes. So I'd go on home with her. Well, *you* know how long Mr Charlie stands for *that*, man. Inside a week I was fired.

The second thing I lost was weight. Inside a month I was down from one five five to one O five, man. I got so poorly and rickety I looked like a walking sage-brush. Before breakfast, after breakfast, before lunch, during lunch . . . and what I mean, them meals won't no hellraisers, neither! When I lost my hustle she took to bringing me little snips and snaps from Mrs Charlie's kitchen, you dig? Listen to this, will you? I was meant to sur*vive* on them little chicken legs and itsy-bitsy slices of meringue pies and cupcakes—*you* know what Mr Charlie eats—that she was bringing me. Ain't that a killer for you? I needed *collard* greens, man, and chitluns and hamhocks and kidney beans and rice, y'understand what I'm talking 'bout? Oysters and

eggs, man! . . . not them little snipsnaps *she* was
bringing . . .

You might not believe it, but long about that time I got
to looking for James Turner. I looked for that freckle-face
nigger all over town. I asked the barkeepers, the cafékeep-
ers, cathousekeepers, the floorsweepers . . . man, I searched
*every*wheres for that nigger and do you know what I found
out? That man had not only left town, Jack, he'd done left
the entire STATE! Suzie Q. damn near drove that kat clean
out the *country,* man!

So I had to give it up. I hated to do it, Daddy, believe
me, but I *had* to give it up. And then—dig this final touch,
man—once I gave it up, naturally I didn't have no bread
or nothing and I couldn't find a hustle, so I took to picking
up little things that didn't belong to me. Every living man
and beast knows the end of *that* story: BLAM! Rock piles,
Jackson. Six solid months.

I ain't been the same man since. Life is a bitch, ain't it?
When I got out I hit the railroads. And I'm still riding,
Pops. Still riding. It was too much. Just too much.

OLD MAN MAYPECK

'The only thing wrong with Old Man Maypeck,' my daddy said to me one time, 'is that when he gets to talking there just ain't no stopping him.' Another time he said, when I'd asked him something about the old man, 'That nigger's crazier than a bow-legged coon dog. Don't you go listening to everything that man says, Aaron. He's crazy.'

For a long time I didn't have the chance to prove whether my father was right or wrong, because the old man didn't have much to say to us younger ones. Besides, he didn't like the fact that my father had left my mother. Every time he saw me on the street after that he'd either look the other way or nod his head jerky-like and walk on.

This morning when I was on my way to buy groceries for my father I didn't expect him to say much more than good morning when I passed his house—if that much. The house was right at the edge of town, smack alongside of the dirt road that leads to Kapalachee. It was a nice two-story house that one of his sons built for him. He had two sons in real estate, and I've been told that it was him that had the business before his sons. If you pass by the house early

71

enough in the morning you can see him in the front yard sweeping up with a sage-brush. As I was walking by I saw him cleaning up, just as I thought he would be, so I said good morning.

'Up mighty early, ain't you, Lil One?'

'Yes, sir.'

'Had coffee?'

'No, sir.'

'Come on in and have some.'

I was surprised that he'd asked me in, and the first thing I thought of was what my father'd told me. I thought of making some kind of excuse, but it was too late. He'd already gone inside.

There wasn't much you could tell about Old Man Maypeck. Some folks said he was seventy-five, others claimed he was closer to ninety, and a lot of people said he was a hundred years old. Some folks said his daddy was a white man, others that he was an Indian, and a lot of people claimed he was lying about the whole thing.

Until I was about twelve years old I thought he had only one suit to his name. I thought, too, that that red scarf he wore summer rain or winter was the only one he had to his name. But my father told me that the old man had plenty of clothes, all the same kind: black suits, black shoes, black socks, white stiff-collared shirts and red polka-dot scarves. He had an eggshell-coloured Panama hat, too, but he only wore that in the summertime.

I thought, too, as I was going into the house, that the malacca cane he always carried was the only one he had. But as I went in the front door there was a whole string of them hanging white and neat on a walking-stick rack. It was nice and cool inside and I couldn't smell anything except the coffee brewing; not like most people's houses I'd been in. There was a big straw mat on the floor and not a chair in sight; only a long, low couch against a white-washed wall and a mahogany table in front of it. There was one picture on the wall above the couch—I meant to say a painting—of an old white man with sea-blue eyes and jet-white hair. It was the onliest thing in the way of deco-ration in the room.

For an old man he got around right smartly. When he started taking out the coffee cups and things I offered to help him, but he said no. He set a coffee can and cups and saucers on the table, then he went into the kitchen and brought out a big plate of hot biscuits, butter and bacon. (I found out later that he had a woman that fixed his meals for him every day.) Didn't neither of us say a word for a while. When he started talking it was so sudden-like that I jumped. But I listened real good.

'All this land is mine. All of it. What this here whole town is built up on is my land. It's mine because Old Mis-tress willed it to me when she died. Them high-fashioned stores on Willard Street what me and you can't set a foot in is built up on my land. The Post Office is where the big house used to be, and if you look right close you can still see the foundations of it as you turn the corner of Davis Street. I was borned in that house, and lived in it right along with Old Master and the Mistress. My daddy was white—that's him up there on the wall—and my mammy was a black woman named Janey. My daddy was named John Maynard Peck and he was first cousin to my master, what was Thomas Peck. The niggers took to calling me

"Maypeck" during 'construction days, but I signs my name George Maynard Peck. There was a whole scandalization because of me, which I ain't going to talk about, but this is my land.

'It don't grieve me none that they taken my land. That was the way they was raised. The poor white trash was raised to believe that they's a heap better than the niggerfolks, and the niggerfolks was told in 'construction days that they's every bit as good as the next white trash. So what you's got now is a bunch of poor white trash trying their damndest to be as good as or better than a bunch of scared niggers. That there is the scrucial junction of the entire transaction. But don't let them fool you, son. The good white folks is mostly gone. I could count you the good white folks in this here State on the fingers of one hand without unfolding my thumb. Them big stores and Cadillacs and banks and things they got in the other part of town don't fool me none a-tall. I knowed their daddies and their granddaddies and their greatgranddaddies; and they was nothing but poor white trash. The Big War was the cause of that. At the end of it most the good white folks freed their niggers and left. Or they just stayed here and died away one by one. They's gone, son. Gone, gone, gone.

'Them was terrible times during the Big War. The big road ran right by Old Master's place, and you could see the 'federate soldiers going by right smartly on they hosses. Later on you could see them straggling back looking tired and bloody and worn-out something terrible. I didn't hardly get no sleep in them days. When Old Master goes off to fight he says, "George?" he says. "I want you to guard this place like it was your own land, your own home." So I stood guard outside the big house most the nights with a flint-lock rifle.

'But it wasn't always like that, son! Oh, no, it wasn't always like that! Before all the foolishness that led up to the Big War us niggers on Marse Peck's place had ourselves a time! They'd be hog-killings and corn shuckings and syrupmakings—and at each and every one of them we'd have ourselves a time! Old Marse would give us a couple of hogsheads of whisky and we'd do the Cake Walk and the Jig and the Sammy Brown—ha! you don't know nothing 'bout that, do you? Them dances you young folks do nowadays couldn't hold a pine torch 'gainst a good jig. The womenfolk would dress up in their fineries and us young bucks would do our best to outdo one another on the boards. Yessir, them was good days.

'But the Big War changed all that. The 'federate soldiers took to coming by the big house and Old Mistress and Young Mistress and one of the nigger womens—I forget now which one it was—would fix they bandages up best they could and us house niggers would feed them. Then the Yankees taken to coming by and Old Mistress had us feed them, too, even though she was crying the while. The Yankees didn't bother our place like they did some of the others, because Old Mistress was good to them. Lots of times they'd wreck a place real good and run off with the corn and hosses and turn the niggers loose.

'I remember one day in particular. A bunch of Yankee soldiers come by, and they had some niggers in Yankee uniform with them what did they heavy work. They was bivouacked down by a creek—that same creek that Mutton

Head was drowned in a few years back—and me and another nigger named Cyrus used to take their victuals to them in big, black cookpots. If I don't disremember they'd done been with us three or four days by this time. Well, sir, me and Cyrus was going down the hill towards them this day with this here cookpot slung on a pole between us. When we am about sixty or seventy yards from them a shell lights ka-CHOO-eey right in they midst and niggers and Yankees and bosses and cooterments went every-which-a-way. Cyrus dropped his end of the pole and run like a jackrabbit. I was mighty scared myself, but the trans-action happened so fast I didn't know which way to turn. I was a big buck nigh on to twenty-two years of age at the time, but it looks to me now that that was the first time I thought in my whole life. (Old Master used to say, "You does the work and I does the thinking." Hhhhh-*ha*!) I set down my end of the pole and thought: now what is these white folks killing up one another for? What is it that make a man act like that? I ain't found the answer to that yet, son. I picked up the pole and the cookpot and started back to the big house, because it 'curred to me that my place was by the Mistress. Them Yankees and niggers down yonder had gone to glory.

'The devilment started during 'construction days. The Klux took to killing up and beating up niggers, and most of us was scared spotless. The Yankees took to acting up, too, putting foolishness in niggers' heads. They'd stop a nigger and say, "What's your name?" The nigger would give only his first name, most the times, because a whole heap of them didn't have no last name. So they'd ask the nigger his master's last name and tell him that was his name, too.

Top of that they'd say, "Don't let nobody call you a nigger. You's a Negro." But to this day a nigger to me is still a nigger. Them damn Yankees can go to hell.

'A heap of niggers won't satisfied with their last names. They took to calling themselves big names. I knowed a nigger back then what called hisself Conscrucious Thaddemoseus Frobinnigus Jones. Big, black buck of a nigger he was, nearbout taller than I am and I'm a good six foot two. He was a "Negro". Call him a nigger and he'd be after your butt with a pick-axe. He allowed as how he knowed everything, because he'd done set in court and listen to the Yankee lawyers argue. He got hisself elected to office, and a more uppity nigger you couldn't find twixt here and the Commonwealth of Virginia. Ask him a question, say you ask him, "Mr Frobinnigus, sir, what do the word 'trial' mean?" He'd rear his shoulders back and say, "That there is the animosity of the scrurrilous elements of propitiosity over the irrigational tragedy of the plexus."

'It was a tragedy, alright. A *great* tragedy. Here was a bunch of niggers what couldn't tell you the difference between a summons and a persimmons elected to office over the few intelligent white folks what was left in the State. I hear tell you's being sent to school up North.'

'Sir?'

'I said I hear tell you's being sent to school up North.'

'Yes, sir. North Carolina.'

'Young Master was killed in North Carolina. My daddy was killed at Bull Run. Eat up, son. Have some more biscuits.'

'Thank you, sir.'

'How's your coffee?'

'Sir?'

'What's the matter, son? Losing your hearing? Have some more coffee.'

'My daddy said I wasn't to drink but one cup a day,' I said. The old man didn't even look at me. When he'd poured me another cup he went on.

'Old Master come back from the war looking mighty poorly. He'd lost twenty pounds at the least, and his skin was right yellowish. He'd had the fever. There won't a nigger on the place what won't glad to see him back safe, because we was all mighty liking to Old Master. One day he gathered all the niggers in front of the big house—there was a conch shell what the supervisor used to blow—and he says, "Today you is as free as I is. That is the law of the land. You is free to stay on here and work for wages, or you is free to go wheresomever you please. The choice is yourn. Do what you think best, and God bless you all." Then he goes inside the house with tears rolling down his cheeks.

'The niggers didn't know what Old Master means. Some of them thought he'd done gone plumb crazy. They all got to whispering to one another; then the field niggers ambled on back to the field like they always did, and the house niggers got to crying and hollering. That night they held a meeting 'mongst theyselves. Out of the one hundred and fourteen peoples Old Master had, eighty-four elected to stay on and work for him, with or without wages. The rest of them went North. My black mammy and two half-brothers went North and I ain't seen or heard a word from them since. But to this day I can tell a field nigger from a house nigger. Field niggers walk like they ain't got a care in the world, and house niggers is right nervous and prissy-like, most like a white man. You is a house nigger. Eat up, son.

'Don't you be letting nobody put no race problem foolishness in your head up North; else you'll be just like Conscrucious. The first thing you got to learn about the race problem is that there ain't no race problem. People ain't like cattle or hosses what you can breed and put labels on. And people ain't like cattle or hosses what you can own, neither. Can't no man own no other man, son. He can *think* he owns him, but he can't own him. Ask any white man alive what freedom is and the first thing he'll do is set down and write a book about it. Eat up, son, I got things to do,' the old man said, and stopped talking just as suddenly as he'd started. As I was leaving he said, 'On July 14th, 1940, I'll be a hundred and one years old; so I ain't got much longer to stay on God's earth. It's all yours, son. It's all yours.'

When I got home my father said, 'Where you been all this time, Aaron?'

'I been over at Old Man Maypeck's,' I said.

'Didn't I tell you that old man is crazy?'

'Yes, sir,' I said. 'You sure did.'

SCHOOLDAYS
IN NORTH CAROLINA

*I. My Arrivance at Tillson Academy, and the Greetings
from my Fellow Students and Old Lady*

It was the first time I'd been driven anywhere by a white man in my life, and it felt funny. It was hot inside the car. The windows were rolled up and there was a film of tobacco dust on the glass. We'd stopped at an intersection while a line of long-distance trucks rolled by, and it seemed there was no end to them. I looked into the rearview mirror and the driver's eyes met mine. His skin was the colour of a faded pink rose, and his eyes didn't have any expression in them at all, just grey and flat and staring. We sat there, both of us, looking into each other's eyes while the motor idled. Then he said, in a voice as flat as his eyes, 'You can roll the window down if you want. It's cooler that way but it lets the dust in.'

I rolled the window down and the dust came in.

There was a filling station across the street from us, and an old negro in coveralls was sitting on the kerb of it playing with a mongrel dog. I'd gotten off the train a few minutes earlier and walked down a gravel platform that led to the dirt road we were on now. My suitcase was heavy. When I got to the road I saw the driver standing beside his car with his foot on the front fender. I looked around for a taxi with a coloured driver, but there weren't any in sight. I started down the dirt road, lugging the suitcase, and when I was abreast of the driver he said, 'Where you going, boy?'

'I want to go to the Tillson Academy,' I said.

'You mean Susan Weber?'

'No,' I said. 'The Tillson Academy.'

'Get in.'

I got in. Watching the old negro and the dog, now, I wondered whether the driver knew where he was going, and whether I should have gotten in at all. My heart began to beat a little faster.

The last of the trucks went past. The driver started off right sudden-like and as we passed the filling station the car almost hit the mongrel dog. The old negro said 'Hey!' and jumped out of the way. My heart beat faster still. We turned off the dirt road on to a paved road, and then through an archway with brick pillars on either side of it. On one of the pillars the words 'Susan Weber Tillson Memorial Academy' were carved in cement. My heart beat easier. The driver stopped the car in front of a long, two-storied brick building, and there were boys in orange and black football gear scrimmaging on the lawn in front of it. When they saw the taxi they stopped and watched me get out. I paid the driver and when I turned around to pick up my suitcase I saw that they were lined up along the stone path that led from the street to the steps of the dormitory. My heart began to beat fast again. I picked up my suitcase and started up the path.

'Is the—I mean is this the Tillson Academy?' I said, feeling nervous and foolish at the same time.

'No,' somebody said. 'This is Princeton.'

'Where're you from, nigger?'

'I'm from New York,' I said.

Somebody giggled.

'Whereabouts in New York you from, son?'

'A hundred and twenty-seventh street,' I said.

'That nigger's from Arkansas,' somebody said. 'You can tell an Arkansas nigger by the way his ears wiggle when he lies. Y'all see that nigger's ears wiggle right then?'

Everybody nodded.

'What's your name, son?'

'Aaron Jessup,' I said.

'Is your mother's name Jessup?'

'Don't put that boy in the dozens,' somebody said.

'Aaron's mother couldn't make the grade,' another boy said, 'but when she got to Tillson she had it made!'

They all laughed.

'What does your mother call you, boy?'

'Back home they call me Lil One,' I said.

'Listen to that nigger talk about "back home". If that nigger's from New York I'm the President of Peru. Tell us where you're from, nigger, sure enough.'

'New York,' I said.

'Let's see your teeth,' somebody said. 'The only way to tell where a nigger is from is to look at his teeth. Show your teeth, son.'

I showed my teeth.

'Ooooooh-wee! *Look* at them pretty white teeth! Don't *nobody* but Georgia niggers have teeth like that. How old're you, son?'

'Fifteen.'

'Fifteen years old and healthier'n a coon in the spring-time. Let's sell the son of a bitch.'

'How much you reckon you'd bring, boy?'

'I don't know,' I said.

'That nigger's worth at least three hundred dollars,' somebody said.

'Three hundred dollars! That nigger'd bring at *least* a thousand. What would you do if you was caught with a white woman in Georgia, son?'

'Die,' I said.

They all laughed real loud, then little by little they drifted back to the lawn and started passing the football around.

When I got inside the dormitory I saw that there was a door just to the right of the entrance with a sign on it that read OFFICE. I knocked. A woman opened the door and said, 'Oh. You must be Mr Jessup. Come in.'

I went in.

'Did Mr Jefferson meet you at the station?'

'No, ma'am.'

'He didn't?'

'No, ma'am.'

She was a light-skinned woman a little older and a lot fatter than my mother. Her ankles were very thick, so that when she walked it looked as though she waddled. There were lots of papers on a big desk in the centre of the room and while she fumbled among them she said, 'I told him we had a boy coming in on the afternoon train. He must have forgotten.' She had a nice voice.

She was still fumbling among the papers, so I looked around the room. There were photographs on the walls of boys and girls in graduation gowns. Beneath the photographs, in neat white letters, were the words Class of 1936, Class of 1929, Class of 1937, and so forth.

'I'm Mrs Washington, by the way, and I'm the Matron,' the woman said. And then: 'Ah, here it is. I have a letter here from your father.'

'Yes, ma'am,' I said. 'I wrote it.'

She looked at me right quick, over her glasses, and we both knew it wasn't the thing to've said. As I shifted from one foot to the other I could see her thinking of something to replace what she'd intended to say. 'This is a Presbyterian school,' she said after a while, 'and the rules are pretty strict. Study hour is from seven to ten and no one is allowed out of their room during that period. Lights go out at eleven.' She stopped, like she was thinking, then went on: 'We had to send a few boys home last year for cutting up and carrying on. You wouldn't want that to happen to you, would you?'

'Oh, no, ma'am!' I said.

'Very well. Here's the key to your room.'

I said thanks, took the key, and went outside. The brass number on the key was 210, so I started up to the second floor. The building was old and the wooden stairs were wearing thin in the middle. But it was clean and it wasn't as hot as it was outside. Way down the hall, on the second floor, I could hear two boys laughing. I set my suitcase down in front of the door of Room 210 and put the key in the lock. As I started to turn the key the door opened right sudden-like and a boy about my age stuck his head out.

'What the hell you doing?' he said.

'I live here,' I said.

'Oh,' he said, and opened the door. 'You going to be my old gal?'

'Your who?'

'My old gal. Down here we don't say room-mate, we say "old gal" or "old lady". Come on in.'

I picked up my suitcase and went inside. The room was just a little bigger than the one I lived in at home. There was a double-decker bed on one side, and opposite it a long desk with a chair at either end. And there was a small armchair under a lamp in the corner near the window.

'My name's John Davis,' the boy said, 'but everybody calls me "Geechie".'

I told him my name and my nickname and he said, 'Don't bother about unpacking now. Put your stuff in the corner. You're from New York, huh?'

'Yeah,' I said. 'How'd you know?'

'I heard you talking to the guys downstairs.'

'Oh,' I said.

'You know Bert McCleoud?'

'No.'

'Which bed do you want? I like the lower. Squirt Thompson?'

'What?'

'You know Squirt Thompson?'

'No.'

'Jimmy Clark?'

I still had the doorkey in my hand, and all these questions were confusing me. I put the key away and said, 'Who's Jimmy Clark?'

'They're all from New York,' Geechie said.

'Who?'

'Bert McCleoud and Squirt Thompson and Jimmy Clark.'

'Oh,' I said again.

'I'm from Rock Hill,' Geechie said. 'Ever hear tell of it?'

'Rock Hill, South Carolina?'

'Yeah!'

'Sure I heard tell of it.'

'Most people from New York ain't never heard tell of it. You want the lower bed? I'll flip you for it.'

'It don't make that much difference,' I said. 'You can have it if you want.'

'Thanks,' Geechie said. We liked each other, and it was a good feeling. I put my bag in a corner like he'd said a long time before that I should. While I was doing it I got to thinking that maybe I couldn't answer all the questions the guys from New York might ask, so I said, with my back to Geechie, 'I ain't from no New York. I'm from Alabama.'

'Are you, sure enough?' Geechie said. He didn't sound surprised or anything, so I turned and looked at him. He was picking his nails.

'That ain't nothing,' he said without looking at me. 'When I first come to Tillson I was from Newark, New Jersey.'

We both laughed.

'You got any brothers and sisters?'

'I got a brother and a sister,' I said. 'My sister's the one that lives in New York.'

'You the baby?'

'Yeah. How about you? You got any brothers and sisters?'

'I got two sisters.'

'And a mother?' I said.

'Son of a bitch,' Geechie said, and we laughed again. 'What grade're you in?'

'Tenth.'

'So'm I. You play football?'

'No.'

'Baseball?'

'No.'

'Basketball?'

'No.'

'What the hell do you do? Jack off?'

'Hell,' I said. 'How 'bout you; you play anything?'

'Football.'

'First team?'

'Second. Come on over here.'

He got up from the lower bed and I followed him over to the window. He put one foot up on the radiator and said, 'See that building over there?' He was pointing to a brick building about fifty yards away from the one we were in. When I said yes he said, 'That's the administration building. See the one in back of it?'

'No.'

'I don't mean directly in back. Look over there to the left. See it? I could just barely see a corner of it sticking up behind the trees. 'That there's the girls' dormitory,' Geechie said. The gymnasium is right across the street from it, but you can't see it from here. You want to look around?'

'I'd like to wash up first,' I said, 'then I have to send a telegram.'

'Alright,' Geechie said, 'I'll walk you into town. The bathroom at the other end of the hall is cleaner than the one at this end.'

'Thanks,' I said. Then I thought a while and said, 'I mean thanks, old gal.'

Geechie smiled.

Later on we walked up the dirt road the taxi driver had taken when he brought me to the school. We turned right at the intersection and walked up the highway which formed the main street of the town. It was almost as small as the one I live in in Alabama, and looked a lot the same, too. There were white frame houses on either side of the street and as we passed restaurants and cafés we could see signs in the windows that read 'For White Only' or 'For Ladies and Gentlemen Only'. In the centre of the town, in the main square, there was a statue of a Confederate soldier standing on a pedestal, just as there is in the town I live in. The main difference between the two towns, I thought as I looked around, was that in this one all the cars had North Carolina licence plates.

I sent the telegram—Arrived Safe Love Aaron—and Geechie and I went back to the campus. Geechie didn't take me to the coloured section of town because he said I'd see enough of that before the school year was over. The school itself was in the white section of town, just as the school church was. We went to the home economics building and the gymnasium and the workshop, where carpentry was taught. I liked the place. I liked it a whole lot, even more than I thought I would. And I was glad that Geechie was my old lady and not one of the boys I met when I first arrived.

II. Saturday Mornings, When They Worked the Dump Truck and I First Saw Her

I don't like to work, and I avoid it whenever I get the chance. Most of us had work to do to pay part of our tuition, and one of my jobs was to help out on the Saturday morning dump truck. It was an old, rickety Ford with sides to it but no tailgate, and when the motor was started it sounded like an aeroplane. We called it 'The Black Goose', because the bus the football team went to games in was called 'The Blue Goose'.

This particular Saturday morning there were five of us on the truck. There was Geechie, myself, Squirt Thompson, Jimmy Clark, and a tall boy from Fredericksburg, Virginia, named Anderson Trayford. We called him 'Lightning'. The truck was parked right in front of the boys' dormitory. The boys who weren't working that morning were all in their windows yelling down at us, and we talked about their mothers in no uncertain terms. When Mr Jefferson came out of the dormitory we stopped yelling. Mr Jefferson was the one that drove the truck. He got into the cab and turned the ignition on. The motor wouldn't budge. He tried it again. It sounded like a siren that had got stuck and couldn't go any higher. He put his head out the window and said, 'One o' y'all come on out here and crank it.'

'Go ahead, old gal,' Geechie said.

'Hell,' I said. 'Why don't you?'

'Send Lightning,' Jimmy Clark said. He pushed Lightning and Lightning made as if to hit him, playful-like.

'Hurry up back there,' Mr Jefferson said. 'We ain't got all morning.' Squirt jumped off the truck and took the crank from Mr Jefferson and cranked the truck up. The motor started, sputtering, and Squirt handed the crank back to Mr Jefferson and jumped back on to the truck. The boys in the windows clapped and yelled, and Squirt thumbed his nose at them. Jimmy Clark started whistling a Jimmy Lunceford tune, and the rest of us picked it up. When the truck started off we were all singing and shouting:

> Tain't what you do
> it's the way how you do it,
> That's what ge-ets results.

Holding on to the sides of the truck and screaming like girls as it turned the corner, then going on with the tune,

> You can try hard,
> don't mean a thing.
> Take it easy, GREEE-sy,
> then the jive can swing . . .

shouting at the top of our voices as the truck stopped in front of the administration building. Geechie and Lightning and myself got off and put three trash barrels filled with paper on to the truck, then we started off again. The next stop was the

gymnasium, then we drove around to the back of the girls'
dormitory. This was the biggest building on the campus,
because there were almost twice as many girls as there were
boys in the school. There were three floors to it, and a large
basement that held the school dining-room.

Lots of girls were leaning on the sills behind the screens
in their windows. Some of them were smiling and others
were just looking at us. I was about to help load the trash
barrels on to the truck when I saw her. She had long, black
hair curling down around her shoulders, but what with the
screen and all I couldn't see her face properly. So I walked
over and stood below her window, which was on the first
floor just above the kitchen. As I stood there looking up at
her it looked to me like she was saying 'yes' with her eyes.
I didn't know yes what; just yes. I thought she was the
prettiest girl I'd ever seen; even prettier than Maybelle, the
first girl I ever loved. I just stood there, looking at her,
much as a starving man would a ripe orange that's just out
of his jumping reach.

'I'm going marry you,' I said.

She laughed as if she'd been goosed. 'You and who else?'
she said.

'Me myself and I,' I said. 'I'm going marry you.'

'You're crazy, boy.'

'I ain't crazy. What's your name?'

'Don't you know?'

'Should I?'

'Yes, you should.'

'I wish I did. Why don't you tell me?'

'My name's Del.'

'Del what?'

'Del Adams.'

'What grade're you in?'

'Same as you. I take Chemistry with you.'

'Do you? I ain't never—' I started to say, then I remembered: that day in Chemistry class when I dropped my pencil. It fell behind my chair, and when I stooped to pick it up I saw that I could see up the dress of a girl sitting behind me; a pretty girl. I looked up her dress and picked up the pencil then looked at her face. She was smiling, with the corners of her mouth turned down, just as she was now. 'I ain't never seen you there,' I said.

'Haven't you?' she said, still smiling in that funny way.

'Come on, Lil One, give us a hand,' Mr Jefferson yelled.

'Not that I remember,' I said to the girl.

'Lil One, you going give us a hand?' Mr Jefferson said. He was getting cross.

'I'm coming,' I said. And then to the girl: 'I'll see you around.'

'In Chemistry?' she said, and laughed. I tried to laugh back, but the corners of my lips were trembling. So I said, 'Yeah, I reckon so,' and went over and helped with the trash barrels.

She was nearbout the first person I saw when I went to lunch that day. The door that the boys entered the dining-room from was at the front end of the building, at the end of the walk that led down from the gymnasium across the street. As you enter from this door the first two tables are the training tables, which is where the athletes sit. Many of them wore black turtle-neck sweaters with orange *T*s on their chests. At the other tables, on both sides of the aisle, were negroes of every shade of humanity under the sun, from near-white to near-black. I was the second boy in the dining-hall on this day I'm telling you about. Smitty (the boy who put me in the dozens the first day I arrived—I thought of him that way for about a year) was ahead of me. He was a star football player, so he sat at the first table. As I passed him I slapped him lightly on the back of his head, and when I looked around he was shaking a finger at me and laughing. Then I saw Del.

She was sitting on the other side of the aisle, about three tables back from the one I sat at. When I looked at her she smiled, then turned away. Oh, God, she was beautiful!

I sat at the same table with my play mother. She was a pretty girl from Hillsboro, North Carolina, and she was three years older than me. Her name was Dolly Simpson. When I sat down I said, 'How you doing, play mamma?'

'Fine, Lil One,' she said. 'You're early today.'

'For a change,' I said. 'You know Del Adams?'

'You like her?'

'It ain't a question of that. You know her?'

'She's right cute.'

'Where's she from?'

'Right here in town.'

'How come she's boarding out if she lives here in town?' I said.

'She lives with her uncle. He ain't married, so he boarded her out. You like her?'

'Hell,' I said. Dolly took a slice of bread from the platter in front of her and tore a piece from the middle of it. We had a private joke about that, so when she looked at me through the hole in the slice of bread we laughed. 'You like Del?' she said again.

She's nearbout as cute as you are,' I said.

Dolly laughed. 'Don't be jiving me, little nigger,' she said. 'I'm your play mother.'

Most of the people that sat at our table were already in their place by this time. Dolly said, so that everybody could hear, 'My play son's in love.'

'Is my old gal in love, sure 'nough?' Geechie said.

'He sure is that,' Dolly said.

'Hell,' Lightning said. 'A piece o' trim and a glass of cold water would kill that boy deader than John Wilkes Booth.'

We all laughed loud. The dining-room matron rapped on her table, and we quieted down. When everyone else in the room was quiet, the girl who was appointed to lead the singing started off and we all joined in and sang grace. While we were singing, with heads bowed, I kept wondering what would happen if I went over and kissed Del. *Del, Del, Del*, I kept thinking. *Del.*

When grace was over and the girls appointed as waitresses began bringing the food in, Lightning said, 'Who's going to the show this afternoon?'

'What's on?' Jimmy Clark said.

Del.

'A shoot-em-up,' Lightning said.

'I'm going,' I said. 'That is, if my old gal lends me a dollar.'

We all giggled, because Geechie was famous for being the tightest boy in school. He wouldn't lend his ageing mother a dime, let alone anybody else a whole dollar.

'Y'all go to hell,' Geechie said.

'Who's in it?' Squirt said.

'Paulette Goddard and somebody,' Lightning said. 'It's supposed to be pretty good.'

Del.

'Ain't no such thing as a good Western,' Dolly said.

'Who's in it besides Paulette Goddard?' Geechie said.

'Ain't no such thing as a good Western,' Dolly said again. 'I wouldn't give a hootch who's in it.' She turned to me. 'I bet Lil One would like to be a movie star, wouldn't you, Lil One?'

'Hell,' I said.

'Lil One's in love,' Jimmy Clark said. 'Nix on being a movie star. Right, Lil One?'

'Y'all go to hell,' I said.

'Who's in it besides Paulette Goddard?' Geechie said again.

'Y'all see these all-negro movies Hollywood's putting out?' Squirt said.

'Yeah,' Dolly said. 'They all look as if they'd fall over dead if you much as looked at them too hard.'

'Who's in it besides Paulette Goddard?' Geechie said for the third time.

'Del Adams is in it,' Dolly said, and looked at me. 'Del Adams is in it.'

Del.

III. *After the Lights Were Out*

Most times me and Geechie didn't go to sleep right after the lights were out. We'd talk, sometimes, about girls, or about what it was like to live in Rock Hill, South Carolina, or a small town in Alabama. And just because we had to turn the lights out didn't mean we couldn't play the radio real low if we wanted to. Geechie had a good radio, but sometimes we'd have to slap it hard before it would work right. So we'd lie in bed, some nights, and listen to the radio; and when it blinked out we took turns at getting up and slapping it.

Saturday nights Squirt and Lightning and Bert McCleod and Jimmy Clark would come into our room after lights out, and we'd listen to the radio and drink Pepsi Colas. If we were lucky we would get Glenn Miller or Tommy Dorsey or Artie Shaw, and if we were *real* lucky we would get Earl Hines or Count Basie or Erskine Hawkins. When the broadcasts came from New York or New Jersey we couldn't get them very clearly, so we'd crowd around the radio in a bunch, and when it blinked out we'd curse and slap it. Sometimes it would blink out in the middle of a real fine solo, and we'd all groan as if we were mortally wounded. Every time this happened Geechie would swear he'd get it fixed the next Monday, but he never did.

Some nights we wouldn't talk at all. Geechie would be tired and fall right off to sleep and I'd climb down from my bed and try to get Count Basie or Jimmie Lunceford; and when I couldn't I'd turn the radio off and climb back into bed. When I closed my eyes I could see myself as a band-leader at the Apollo Theatre in New York, all dressed up in a double-breasted white suit that would change to red or green or purple as the lights flashed on it. I'd have a baton in my hand, just like Jimmie Lunceford, and the announcer would say, 'And now, ladies and gentlemen, the main attraction of our show, Aaron Jessup and his orchestra!' and everyone would clap and whistle and I'd give the downbeat and the band would break into our theme-song, a real swinging one, and the transparent curtains would part and the whole stage would move forward as it does in big New York theatres. Other times I'd see myself as a star soloist, like say Lester Young or Chu Berry, and when it came time for my solo I'd ease myself out of the orchestra real slow, like Lester Young does, and walk up to the microphone and hold my sax way off to the side and say, 'Toot! Boot! Boodle-oodle-oodle-deet!' and the band would answer 'Cha-dat DAH-da' and the kats in the balcony would shout 'Yeah!'

Then I could see myself backstage after the show, signing autographs, and a real pretty girl would come up to me and say, 'What you doing later on, Aaron?' and I'd be real casual and say, 'I'm sorry, baby, but I'm busy', and she'd weep and gnash her teeth like they say in the Bible.

Susan Weber Tillson was an abolitionist, and she lived in Boston. When she died she left a heap of money to the school, and there was a large picture of her in the auditorium of the administration building. Sometimes when I closed my eyes, after lights out, I would try to think of Del but instead of Del I would see Susan Weber Tillson smiling at me with her hair parted straight down the middle and combed down on each side of her forehead, smiling white and pretty, and I'd try hard to see Del but I couldn't so I'd open my eyes and stare into the dark. When I closed them again I could see myself as Susan Weber's husband, with wavy black hair and sideburns and a full dress suit and when we went to bed we slept in the same bedroom, not in different bedrooms like I hear most white people do. I'd think then that someday maybe I could go out to Hollywood and be a chauffeur for a beautiful movie star (please God) and she'd say oh Aaron, Aaron, Aaron my *dearest* love and I'd do that to her too because they say women love you for the rest of your natural life once you do that to them and later we'd drive out to the Boulevard with her in the back seat and I'd stop the car and get out and open the door for her and say 'Ma'am' and wouldn't a living soul know the difference. Then I'd look to see if Geechie was asleep and when was Del would come into the room and she'd say Aaron, Aaron, Aaron, oh Aaron, I *love* you! . . .

And on winter evenings the pine trees would be so heavy with snow that they looked like overgrown ice-cream cones and you could walk along a road you knew was dusty underneath but crusted over now with frozen snow. Once on such a winter evening Geech was with me and we were trying to get back to the dormitory before lights out and we saw a white girl of sixteen or seventeen undressing in a house along the way. I said: 'We better get out of here before something happens.' Geechie said: 'Come on, fool, let's go over and have a look. Nothing will happen.' So we crossed the little lawn cleaned of the day's snow with the grass brown in the moonlight and peeped through the window with our breath coming unnaturally fast as she stripped to what she was born with then started doing something funny to herself and Geechie giggled and we ran as if chased by a pack of bloodhounds and when we'd caught our breath sufficiently to talk Geechie said 'Ooooh-wee!' and then 'You like white women?' and I said 'Yeah, hell yeah, if they're pretty' and he said 'You like one enough to *die* for her?' and I said 'No' and we got to the dormitory just as the doors were closing.

I used to think about that, too, after the lights were turned out.

IV. *Sir Francis Drake,*
the Boot Fleet, and a Handful of Roses

Jimmy Clark and me used to sit side by side on the back row of our History class. Jimmy's seat was right next to the window, and when we got bored we would look out at the faculty children playing on the steps of the gymnasium across the street. Then, in the spring of my first year at Tillson, we made up a game called 'The Ofays and the Boots'. It went like this: we'd take a battle—almost any battle—and refight it with a box of matches. Jimmy would take out a box of matches and hand me half of them, and we'd hold our hands beneath our seats and break them in two. The ones with black tips were the Boots, and the ones with plain ends the Ofays. We'd line the matches up on a blank page of one of our notebooks which was spread on the arm of Jimmy's desk. Then the battle would begin.

On this particular day—it was a Thursday in April, if I remember rightly—Jimmy looked at me, and I at him. Without a word he took out a box of matches and handed me half of them, and we began breaking them in two. When we were finished Jimmy took one with a black tip and one with a plain tip, mixed them up and held one in each fist. I touched his left fist and got an Ofay. Then we sat back and thought for a while.

'Trafalgar?' Jimmy whispered.

'We fought that last week,' I said. We thought a while longer and then Jimmy said, behind his hand, 'How 'bout the Spanish Armada?'

I nodded.

'The Spaniards are the Boots, right?'

'Right,' I said.

'OK,' Jimmy said. 'I'm the Duke of Medina Sidonia.'

'I'll be Sir Francis Drake,' I said.

We lined the matches up on the blank page, the Ofays at the top and the Boots at the bottom. 'Watch it,' Jimmy said. 'Here come the Boots.' He began moving his first line of matches up the page, one by one. I sat there and watched him without moving any of my own. He kept moving his pieces up, one by one, glancing at me every once in a while. Then, when I still didn't move, he nudged me. 'What the hell's wrong?' he said.

'Tea time,' I said. 'Sir Francis and the boys are juicing it up.'

'Oh, yeah?' Jimmy said, 'BOOM!'

We both giggled.

'Mr Clark and Mr Jessup,' the teacher said, 'if you two aren't interested in what I'm saying you may leave the room.'

We both said how sorry we were, then went on with the game on the sly. I started moving my matches down towards his, and he began moving the pieces up from his back row. When the two front rows were facing each other, with black tips facing blank white ones, we both stopped. I didn't look at Jimmy, because I knew that if I did we'd both burst out laughing. (Every time we got to this point, where the black heads faced plain white tips, we found it hard not to laugh.) Then Jimmy said, 'Ready?' and we both mixed the matches up real fast, saying 'Boom, boom, boom, boom!'

The notebook fell to the floor, and we both looked innocent.

'Mr Clark and Mr Jessup,' said the teacher, 'you may both leave the room.' We picked up our books and went outside.

When we'd gotten over our laughter Jimmy suggested that we go to Hayti—which is what the coloured section of town was called—and listen to records on one of the jukeboxes. I didn't feel like it, so I took Jimmy's books to his room for him and then went to my own room and picked up a Latin text. I studied for a while, then put the book aside and took a letter from my pocket. It was written on notebook paper and folded so that when you opened it a certain way it turned into a boat. I unfolded it and read it for what must have been the tenth time.

Dear Aaron, I have receive your letter of yesterday and also the one of the day before. I am writing this from bed. The sun is shining bright and I wish that I could take a walk into town all by myself like the boys can.

To answer the question of your last letter, I did not look at you in Chemistry because I was Thomas

McC. Henderson's girlfriend and it would not have been fair either to him or to myself. I am always fair to who I am going with at the time, as I think you can see by my actions.

But I have always thought that your a nice guy. And now that Mr Thomas McC. Henderson and myself are not any longer the best of friends I take pleasure in accepting your invitation to the Social this Friday night.

Yours truly, Del Adams.

P.S. I do not see why you do not give your letters to me yourself instead of giving them to Dolly to give to me. After all (smile) your not a shy guy. D.A.

I folded the letter and put it back in my pocket and went downstairs. School was over by this time, and there were about three horse-shoe games going on in back of the dormitory. Bert McCleoud and Lightning were playing on the third landing, so I went over to them.

'Who's winning?' I said.

'Two to one my favour,' Bert said.

'I got the winner,' I said.

'The hell you have,' Lightning said. 'We're playing best four out of seven, World Series style.'

I spread my handkerchief on a stone and sat on it. Then I took the letter from my pocket and read it again. I wondered if I should tell her about the mistake in 'your' for 'you're', and decided I wouldn't. I sat and watched Bert and

Lightning play for a while, then got up and went back upstairs. When I got to my room Geechie was lying in bed reading.

'Where the hell you been?' I said.

'At your mother's house,' Geechie said. 'I hear you got thrown out of class.

'*Parvam puellam accusatis . . .*' I said. 'Finish it.'

'*Quod rosas portant*,' Geechie said.

'*Portant* your nappy head,' I said. '*Portat*.'

'I hear you got thrown out of class.'

'Yeah,' I said. 'Me and Jimmy Clark.'

'What were y'all up to?'

'Just kidding around,' I said. 'I got a letter from Del.'

'Did you, sure enough?'

'I sure did.'

'Let's see it.'

'Hell, no.'

'Come on, old gal, let's have a look-see.'

'Hell, no.'

'What'd she say?'

'She says I'm a good-looking son of a bitch and she loves me better than Juliet loved Romeo.'

'You ugly bastard, what'd she say, sure enough?'

'She says your feet stink and you don't love your Jesus.' Geechie threw a book at me and I caught it and said, 'She says I can see her at the social this week.'

'Nice!' Geechie said. 'Think you can handle it?'

'Handle what?' I said.

'*You* know . . .'

'Hell,' I said. 'I've had more trim than you'll ever have if you live to be a hundred and five.'

'Yeah,' Geechie said. 'And every one of them was named Minnie Fingers.'

'You're a black liar,' I said.

Geechie jumped up from the bed. 'There ain't but three things I hate in life,' he said, shaking a finger in my face. 'Niggers, flies and people who call me a black liar. I got you on two counts, so come on, son, let's get it ON!' We both stripped to the waist, then we pushed the desk and chairs aside and sparred around the middle of the room. It was mostly bobbing and weaving and footwork, because we never hit each other very hard. When we stopped Geechie said, 'I hope you make out, old gal. She's a nice girl.'

Del.

Friday night: I tilted the bureau mirror towards the light so that nothing but my head was showing. Then I took off the handkerchief that I'd wrapped tight around my head to keep my hair down and looked at my hair. It was lying flat, and I squeezed three artificial waves in the front of it with my fingers. There was a crease in my forehead where I'd knotted the handkerchief, and I rubbed it with my hand.

'You old nappy head,' Geechie said. 'Why don't you give up?'

'Go to hell,' I said. I'd hoped he wasn't looking. I set the mirror straight and sat in the armchair. I'd just had my suit cleaned and pressed, and I put the seams of my trousers inside my knees so's not to spoil them. I was afraid I'd spoil them anyhow if I sat down too long, so I got up and stood by the window. *Del.* The lights in the faculty houses across the street were on, and the landscape looked just like I thought the landscapes that Charles Dickens wrote about would look: dark with houses dotted across the hills.

I'd been to a few socials before to see a girl named Artelia Tennessee, but she fell in love with somebody else. I knew that if you got to the social early enough you could get the couch in the corner of the reception room. That was the one the chaperon couldn't see too well, but from which you saw every move she made. I glanced at my watch. Ten more minutes. I started to go across the hall to see if Lightning was ready, but when I got to the door I changed my mind. I went back to the window and put my foot on the radiator.

'You act like an expectant father,' Geechie said.

'You mean like the husband of an expectant mother,' I said.

'Go to hell,' Geechie said.

I took my foot off the radiator and went back to the mirror. I felt the crease in my forehead. It was still there, but you could barely see it. I looked at my hair and thought, 'Damn it, why can't everybody have the same kind of hair a white man has? With this stuff you got to pamper it and pull it and put all kinds of muck on it and it still looks like hell.' There was a banging at the door. Lightning. 'Wait up,' I said, and put my jacket on. When I opened the door Lightning whistled and said, 'Sharper'n a rat turd, son, and that's sharp at both ends.'

'Looking mighty sharp y'self, son,' I said.

'Good luck, old gal,' Geechie said.

'Thanks,' I said. 'See you later.'

Outside in the hall Lightning said, 'What we need is a drink of wine.'

I didn't say anything. I got to thinking of the Harlem Café in Hayti. Geechie and Smitty and Jimmy Clark and I used to go there and listen to the jukebox. Then somebody found out that one of the waiters, a man called Tim Armour, would sell wine in a coke cup if the owner wasn't around. One night I drank three cups and it felt good, real good, but when I got back to the dormitory I got sick. Outside, now, walking towards the girls' dormitory, the same queasy feeling came back and I wished Lightning hadn't said anything about wine. But in a short while it was gone and I was alright. Then I stopped, right sudden-like. 'Lordy!' I said.

'What's the matter?' Lightning said.

'I forgot the flowers.'

I ran back to the dormitory and got them—they were in a glass of water on the windowsill—and when I got back outside Lightning had walked on a little ways, so I ran and caught up to him. Other boys had started over by this time, and it looked just as it looked when we were going to church on Sundays: everybody all dressed up.

Lightning and me walked up the steps to the main entrance of the girls' dormitory. Because I'd had to run back for the flowers we weren't the first ones there. When we were inside I went up to the chaperon and said, 'I'd like to see Miss Adams, ma'am, if I may.' (We had to speak properly to members of the faculty.)

'Miss Del Adams?'

'Yes, ma'am,' I said. I'd forgotten that there were two other girls named Adams. The chaperon rang the buzzer for Del—one long ring for the floor and one, two, three, four for the room: 104. In about half a minute Del came down the hall. She looked gorgeous.

'Hi,' I said.

'Hi.'

'I brought these for you,' I said, and handed her the flowers. She smelled them and smiled. I turned around and winked at Lightning, who was still waiting for his girlfriend, then took Del's arm. When we were inside the reception room the first thing I did was head for that corner couch, but it was already taken. I cursed under my breath and looked around. There was a small love seat not far from the couch, so we went over there and sat down. For a long time neither of us said anything. I just sat there and watched her smell the roses. Lord, she was beautiful!

'What'd you do today?' I said after a while.

'Well,' she said, 'I played volleyball for a while . . .' and stopped. I tried to picture her playing volleyball in shorts, and did. I waited for her to go on but she didn't, so I said, 'What else did you do?'

'This afternoon I ironed. I ironed this dress.'

'You did?'

'Yes.'

'It looks nice.'

'Thanks.'

'I mean *you* look nice. You look beautiful.'

Del looked at me and smiled, then smelled the flowers again. I couldn't think of a thing to say, so I looked around the room. Other boys were talking their heads off, and I wondered how in the world they found that much to say. I sat there for a while, feeling like a fool, then I said, 'I went fishing today.' It was a lie, but I felt I had to say something.

'You did?'

'Yeah.'

'Alone?'

'No. Me and Geechie and Squirt. We went way out to a creek off highway 201. You know the one I mean?'

'No.'

'Well, it's a real big creek, nearbout as big as a river.'

'It is?'

'Yeah.'

'You catch anything?'

'Sure I did. I caught more than anybody else.'

'You *did*?'

'I sure did. I caught seven of them, and the biggest one weighed over a pound. Next time we go out I'll bring you some.'

'What would I do with them?'

'Cook them and eat them!'

'Here?'

'Sure!'

'You know I can't do no cooking here,' Del said.

I hadn't thought about that. I tried to smile, but the corners of my lips were twitching. I broke out into a loud laugh, because I figured that then she wouldn't notice the twitching.

'What you laughing at?'

'I just thought of something real funny,' I said, 'but it ain't for ladies to hear.'

She looked disappointed. Hell, I thought. I looked at the chaperon. She was reading a newspaper. I looked at

Del. She was smelling the roses again, with her lips very close to them. I put my arm around her.

'Don't,' she said, but she didn't move. Her arm was warm and soft and round. I glanced at the chaperon, but she wasn't looking.

'Del,' I said, and pulled her to me. 'Del.'

'Don't,' she said. 'Don't, Aaron. Not here.'

'Del,' I said. 'Just one.'

'Aaron, don't,' she said.

I turned her face to mine and kissed her. Her lips were warm and very moist and I could feel her breath against my cheek.

'Aaron,' she said. 'Stop it.'

I kissed her again, this time with both arms around her. Afterwards we held hands, and her palms were moist. We talked for the rest of the hour—most of it was just chit-chat, but I didn't tell any more lies—and then the chaperon stood up and told us time was up.

'Thanks for the flowers,' Del said. 'They're real pretty.' Her eyes were moist.

'I'm glad you like them,' I said. 'I'll look for you tomorrow at breakfast.'

'Alright,' she said. 'I'll look for you, too.'

I felt right warm inside. 'Good,' I said. 'So long.' We squeezed hands and I went outside. Lightning was waiting for me at the bottom of the stairs.

'How'd you make out, Lover?' he said.

'Pretty good,' I said. We fell into the ragged column of boys walking towards the street. When the lights began to go on in the girls' rooms we turned around and looked. They'd go on one after another, blink, blink, blink, in different parts of the dormitory and on different floors. It was pretty to look at. The girls stood framed in their windows looking down at us, and we waved to them. Some of them waved back with handkerchiefs.

'Oooooh-*wee*!' Smitty said. 'I'd give a million dollars for just one night in that dormitory.'

'Cheap son of a bitch,' Jimmy Clark said. Laughter dribbled up and down the column.

'Y'all see Aaron kiss his girl?' Smitty said.

'Did Lil One kiss Del sure enough?' somebody said.

'*Did* he?' Smitty said. 'That little nigger like to've killed the poor girl.'

Someone started whistling an Erskine Hawkins solo, and most of us joined in. Lightning hit a false note and Smitty said, 'Square. Listen to that square.' Laughter dribbled down the column again. Soon we were near the boys' dormitory, and then inside it. When I got to my room Geechie wasn't there. As I looked out my window I could just barely see the corner of the girls' dormitory behind the dark trees.

Del. Delilov. Delilovyou.

V. Into the Maelstrom of Life

Like I said in the beginning, I don't like to work. But I have to clarify that, because what I meant was manual work. As a consequence I came mighty close to not graduating from Susan Weber Tillson Memorial Academy a-tall. One of the requirements for graduation (for boys) was that you had to complete a course in manual training.

It took me two years to finish a pair of six-inch book-ends that any ten-year-old boy in the whole wide world could have finished in two hours flat. It was only out of the kindness of the manual training instructor's heart that I got a passing grade. I'm here to tell you that that workshop gave your hero hell.

By this time I'd grown a lot, so that now I was about an inch taller than my old gal and almost as tall as Lightning. Our football team did real well that year (which was unusual for Tillson—we usually lost just about every game we played), and our basketball team came out tops in our conference. Everybody was talking about college. Lightning was going to Fisk University in Nashville, Tennessee, the next fall, and Squirt Thompson and Bert McCleoud were going up to Howard. Geechie was thinking of going to Tuskegee Institute, but neither he nor I had made up our minds one way or another.

Del and me were tight by this time. I knew I had the prettiest girl on the campus, and I was mighty proud of it. That last year we tried to arrange it so that we had all of our classes together. We both joined the school choir, too, so that we were together at rehearsals and on long road trips. It was a real fine year all around.

A day or so before graduation the parents began to arrive. Most of them lived right there in North Carolina, to arrive, but a few came from as far away as West Virginia or New Jersey. My father wasn't there because he couldn't afford it, and Geechie's parents weren't there because they had work to do. Lightning's parents came down from Fredericksburg. A strange thing was that once the parents were there we stopped playing the dozens. Even when we were by ourselves.

There were sixty in the graduating class, and twenty-five of us were boys. At the commencement exercises it seemed that the preliminary speeches would never end; and by the time the main speaker was introduced I could hardly keep my eyes open. The main speaker was a very black man who spoke with an English accent. I've forgotten now what his name was. He thanked everyone for being so kind as to permit him to speak at this important occasion, and then he said—this is what I remember best—'On this memorable day, as these young men and women move on to institutions of higher learning, or, as the case may be, into the maelstrom of life——'

'Maelstrom of life.' I got a big kick out of that. When it was all over with and we'd gotten our diplomas I found Del and we went downstairs together.

'Congratulations,' I said.

'Same to you,' Del said. We squeezed hands. I tried to kiss her cheek, but she turned away. 'Not here,' she said. We saw Lightning talking with his parents, so we went over.

'Hey, Lover,' Lightning said. 'Hi, Del.'

We said hello.

'And where will you be going to college, young man?' Mrs Trayford (Lightning's mother) said.

'I don't know, ma'am,' I said.

'Why'nt you come to Fisk, Lover?' Lightning said. 'We'll have a hell—I mean a good time.'

'I'll think about it,' I said.

'You'll do no such thing,' Mrs Trayford said to Lightning. 'You'd better get some knowledge in that big head of yours.' She laughed, looking real pleased with herself and the world in general. Mr Trayford wasn't saying a word, so

I looked at him. He was looking at Del's breasts. From the expression on her face it looked as though she knew it and was getting embarrassed.

'Well,' I said, 'I guess we'll be going.' We said goodbye to Mr and Mrs Trayford, then to Lightning. When we were a little ways off Lightning said, 'See you, Lover! Don't forget to write!'

'I will,' I said. I took Del's hand and we walked across the lawn towards the girls' dormitory.

'What time does your train leave?'

'Not till ten tonight,' I said. 'Are you going home now?'

'In a little while.'

'Now we can get married.'

'Not till I graduate from Hampton.'

'Hell,' I said. 'Now.'

'We have time.'

'Alright. Then we'll have a huge wedding and lots of piccaninnies.'

'Don't call them piccaninnies.'

'Alright. Children.'

'How many will we have?'

'As many as you want. Four, five . . . a hundred.'

Del laughed. 'I love you,' she said. We squeezed hands again, tight, and I stopped.

'Don't be crazy, Aaron,' Del said.

'I'm not crazy,' I said. 'Come here.' I turned her gently towards me and put my arms around her.

'Aaron, darling, don't. There're too many people around.'

'To hell with them. We've graduated, haven't we? Nothing can hap—' I could feel her mouth merged into mine and for a brief second it seemed that she was part of me and I of her.

'Darling, don't,' Del said. She was out of breath. 'Don't, don't.' She covered my lips with her fingers.

'Let's meet at your place,' I said.

'No.'

'Please.'

'My uncle—'

'You said he wouldn't be there. You told me so.' I released her and we began walking again. For a while neither of us said anything. There was a lot of confusion around, as I remember, with boys and girls and parents and teachers all over the place; but Del and I were in a little world of our own.

'You said he wouldn't be there,' I said again. 'He isn't even here. Is he out of town?'

'Yes.'

What with Geechie's and my things scattered all around our room was in a mess. When I got there Geechie was separating his things from mine; we'd worn one another's clothes a lot. He still had his cap and gown on, and was throwing things into an open trunk.

'You look like a priest,' I said.

'Hell,' Geechie said. And then, holding up a tie: 'Is this yours, or mine?'

'Yours,' I said.

He threw the tie into the trunk.

'You about packed?'

'Almost,' I said. 'I've still got lots of time.

I sat on his bed and watched him pack, thinking of all the good times we'd had together. I wanted to tell him how much I'd enjoyed being his room-mate, but I couldn't put what I felt into words. And then, just at that moment, he looked at me and smiled; and I knew he felt the same thing, too. It was embarrassing, in a way; like trying to tell your brother how much you love him.

'Christ,' Geechie said. 'It sure is hot, isn't it?'

'Yeah,' I said. 'It sure is.'

I took off my gown and threw it on top of my bed, then put on my jacket.

'You going someplace?' Geechie said.

'Yeah. I'm going into town.'

'What for?'

'I got things to do.'

'How long will you be gone?'

'I don't know. A couple hours, I guess.'

'A couple hours?'

'Yes.'

'I'll be gone by the time you get back.'

He was holding a pair of trousers that he'd just folded so that he could pack them. We stood there, Geech with the trousers held against the grey gown and me just inside the doorway.

'Well,' Geechie said, 'I guess this is it, old gal.'

'I guess it is,' I said. I could feel a lump rising in my throat. I went over to him and we shook hands, hard.

'So long, gal,' Geechie said. 'Good luck.'

I said goodbye and went outside.

•

I'd never been to Del's house before. It was a neat house with just one story to it. It reminded me a lot of Old Man Maypeck's house back home, because it looked like just the kind of place a single man would live in. The walk leading through the small front yard was swept clean.

I went up the steps to the front door and knocked. Del came to the door in a dress I'd never seen before. Her hair was pulled straight back, and I'd never seen her do that before either. It made her look more like twenty-one than eighteen. She opened the screen door and let me in, then closed it and closed the house door behind it.

'Hi,' she said.

'Hi.'

I took her in my arms and kissed her lips and eyes and ears. I could feel her heart beat against my chest, and for a short while it felt like my own heart switched to the right side of my body. When I turned her loose she said, 'Can I get you something? Tea? Coffee? Anything?'

'Do you have a soda?'

'Yes.'

'I'll have that,' I said.

She got two Pepsi-Colas from the kitchen and came back to the living-room. She handed me one of them and sat in a chair across the room from me. I felt funny. It was like sitting in a room with a strange cat and having it watch everything you do from a quiet corner. I wished then that I was twenty-one or twenty-five or maybe seventy-five. Anything but just plain old eighteen.

'Why don't you come over here?' Del said. I went over and sat on the arm of her chair, but it didn't feel right. I got up and pulled her up by the arms and we kissed.

'Hold me, darling,' she said. 'Hold me tight.'

I held her as tight as I could, and again it felt as if my heart was on the right side of my body instead of the left. I wished then that we could stay there for ever and ever and ever: just locked into each other's arms like that.

'Where's your bedroom?' I said.

'Over there.' She pointed. I lifted her into my arms and we went inside. Then I put her down and kissed her lips and eyes and forehead.

We undressed and got into bed. *God*, she was beautiful! Nothing happened.

'Darling?' Del said.

'Mmm?'

'What's the matter?'

'Nothing.'

'Are you sure?'

'Yes.'

'My darling, my darling,' Del said. I could feel her tears against my cheek. After a time I got dressed and went outside and sat on the steps in the sun.

Del! Oh, Del!

THINK

'Look-a-there!'

'Where?'

'Over there. Look, quick! before she turns the corner.'

'Mmmmm-hmph!'

'She was fine, wasn't she?'

'She sure'n hell was. Look at this one.'

'She ain't so hot.'

'Yeah she is, too. Wait till you see her from the back.'

'. . . Yeah, I see what you mean, Huss.'

'Here come another one.'

'Women sure are fine, ain't they?'

'They sure'n hell are.'

'Tip tip tip-tip tip . . . They sure can walk, can't they?'

'I got a gal over on Lee Street that's finer than that.'

'Finer than *that* one?'

'I'm here to tell you.'

'You been holding out on me.'

'I ain't got to tell you everything, have I?'

'What's her name?'

'I ain't going tell you.'

'What she look like?'

'Fine.'

'I'm hip. But what she *look*, like?'

'Big. She ain't fat; she's just big and *heal*thy.'

'Let's go on over there.'

'To Lee Street?'

'Yeah.'

'The hell you preach.'

''At-*dam*, man, you're the selfishest kat I seen yet. Won't tell me the chick's name, won't tell me what she look like . . . How old is she?'

'Twenty-four.'

'Mellow!'

'I'm here to tell you.'

'Come on, man, let's go over there.'

'*Both* of us?'

'What the hell. You in love with the chick or something?'

'Naw, I ain't in love with her.'

'Then come on. Let's go.'

'Nnn-nnn.'

'How come?'

'She might not like it.'

'You can't never tell unlessing we try, can you?'

'I reckon not. Here come another one. Look-a-there.'

'Mmmmm-*hmph*! I'd sleep in the streets fawdy days and fawdy *nights* . . . Come on, man, let's over to Lee Street.'

'The hell you preach. If I go over there I'm going by myself.'

'How long we knowed one another?'

'Going on six years.'

'Ain't we gone with some of the same chicks?'

'Yeah, but not at the same time.'

'Ain't nothing wrong with that, is it?'

'I ain't thinking 'bout myself. I'm thinking 'bout the chick. She might not like it.'

'Ain't nothing in the books that says she won't.'

'I know, but you can't never tell about womenfolks. Remember Dora?'

'Yeah.'

'I ever tell you about that?'

'No.'

'Remember I used to work as a *ce*ment mixer back then? Well, like I told you, this Dora was the one what used to hand out the pay cheques every week. Cute dark-skin girl she was. Wore her hair in bangs. She used to sit behind a grillework and all you could see was her head. One day I seen her crossing the street—she was ahead of me and I seen her from behind—and it looked to me like the Good Lord had done give her everything he could to provide for the future of the human race.'

'Did you get it?'

'Lemme tell you. That time I won't thinking about hitting on her or nothing like that, y'understand? I already had me a chick and besides, what the hell. There ain't a man alive that gets close to one hundred-thousandth of the chicks he'd like to get close to. So I said to myself, "Well, Huss, that's *one* more you won't get."

'Then one time I seen her at a dance. She was with a tall kat in a corduroy suit. I watched them real close and I seen that he didn't have it made. You can always tell when a man's got it made with a chick. He plays it cool and the chick falls all over him. When he ain't got it made it's the other way around. So when I seen what was happening I moved in.'

'Did you make it?'

'Hush and lemme finish. I made a date with her for the next night at nine, and showed up right on time. She looked so good I felt like hitting on her right then, but I didn't. We just sat around and talked, then I went on home. You see, the way I had it figured was that if I hit on her the first time around she'd get all hinckty and say no. So I cooled it. I saw her again about a week later at my place. I hit on her. She acted like she was the most surprised party in the world, you dig? "Ef I'd known *that* was what you had on your mind I wouldn'ta come over here at all!" she says. I jumped salty. I told her to get the hell out of my place. I never wanted to see her again. She got to crying and carrying on. I was the meanest, orneriest nigger she'd met in her natural life. No, I wasn't. ALL men was like me. She'd never go out with another man as long as she lived: on and on and on. You know what the upshot of *that* rigamarole was, don't you? She ended up staying the night. No, sir. It's just like I said. You can't never tell about womenfolks.'

'That's what I been trying to tell you! Come on, man, let's go see the chick.'

'Naw, man. Suppose the chick jumps salty?'

'So what?'

'"So what" your black butt. If she gets salty then *I'll* be eighty-sixed too.'

'She ain't the only chick you got, is she? Man, you're the *stin*giest kat . . . here you are with all these chicks lined up and I ain't got nothing but fond memories. Come on, man, let's make it!'

'Well . . . awright, what the hell. Come on.'

'Now you're talking.'

'Damn.'

'What's the matter?'

'Sitting on that kerb made my foot go to sleep.'

'Stamp it. Not that way, fool. Kick it. *There* you go. OK now?'

'Yeah. I still don't feel right.'

'Your foot?'

'No. The chick.'

'Aw, *maaaan* . . . you ain't got the right attitude. You got to have the right attitude, man, otherwise you're *hooked*: wedding ring, bells and all.'

'How you know so much? You ain't never been married. It might be fun, for all you know: a nice wife and a house and children . . .'

'I ain't never been married, but my daddy sure was. And I'm here to tell you he was *most* unhappy.'

'Supposing you was one.'

'Supposing I was one what?'

'A woman.'

'Then I'd be a woman, that's all.'

'Yeah, but how would you feel?'

'Feel? I'd feel *great*!'

'How would you feel about eight million hungry kats wanting you all the time?'

'I wouldn't know it, would I?'

'Ha! Don't let Julia fool ya, Pops. *They* know it.'

'Them A-rabs have the right idea. You see one you like, snatch her and put her in a harem.'

'You wouldn't talk like that if you was a woman.'

'Yeah, I reckon you got something there. How would *you* feel if you was a woman?'

'I wouldn't like it worth a good god damn, that's how I'd feel.'

'I bet you'd be right stingy with it, too.'

'If I was a woman?'

'Yeah.'

'No, I wouldn't.'

'Yeah, you would, too. You'd be just like some of these little chicks around here. Act like it's gold or diamonds or something.'

'With kats like you around I reckon they got something there. There's the house.'

'That one over there?'

'Yeah. The one with the curtains blowing.'

'Where's the light coming from?'

'That's her bedroom.'

'She live alone?'

'Yeah.'

'Let's jump through the bedroom window and surprise her.'

'Don't be no fool.'

'I was joking.'

'No you weren't. You're fool enough to pull a trick like that. Watch that front step. It's busted.'

'Thanks.'

'Go ahead. Ring the bell.'

'You ring it. It's your chick.'

'Hmph. Or was.'

'Here she comes. She's stacked, alright.'

'Didn't I tell you? Shh! Here she is.'

'Who is it?'

'It's me, honey. James.'

'Oh. Just a minute. Hi!'

'Hi, honey. I got a friend with me. Henry Baker, Catherine Howard.'

'Hello, Mr Baker.'

'Pleased to meet you, Miss Howard.'

'Won't y'all come in?'

'Thanks, honey.'

'You'll have to excuse the way I look. I didn't think James was bringing anybody with him.'

'You look fine to me, Miss Howard.'

'Oh . . . ha, ha! . . . you're just being nice.'

'No I ain't, neither. You look *real* fine.'

'It's nice of you to say that, but ef I'd known that James was bringing somebody with him I'd have fixed myself up a little.'

'Henry here just got off from work, honey. I met him coming up the street so I thought I'd bring him up for a drink.'

'You're telling a tale, James, and you know it. He's just trying to save my face, Miss Howard.'

'Just call me Catherine.'

'He's just trying to save my face, Catherine. What happened was that we met up like he said and since he'd done told me how fine—I mean how nice you are and all I kind of insisted that he bring me up here. I hope you don't mind.'

'Oh, not in the least! What would y'all like to drink? I ain't got much liquor in the house but I got some beer . . .'

'Beer's fine for me, honey.'

'Nothing like beer on a hot night, Miss Catherine.'

'Alrighty. I'll get some beer. Be right back!'

'She sure is fine.'

'I told you!'

'Yeah, but I didn't think she was *this* fine.'

'Shh! Here she comes.'

'Y'all make yourselves at home. Take your jackets off, if you want.'

'Thanks.'

'Mighty kind of you, honey.'

'Sure is a nice place you got here, Miss Catherine.'

'Just Catherine. It ain't so hot, but at least it's comfortable.'

'You don't need to take it, Miss Catherine, I'll just hang it here in back of the chair.'

'Alrighty. It's a nice jacket.'

'Thanks.'

'I hope the beer's cold enough for you. That icebox don't work too well.'

'Ah! Nothing like beer on a hot night.'

'Or with.'

'What was that, Henry?'

'Nothing. I was just saying that I believe in being informal at all times.'

'You can make yourself at home with Henry around, honey. He's a real old friend. That right, Henry?'

'That's exactly right, my man.'

''Course, now, if we was up North we wouldn't have to worry about the heat. All we'd have to do is go to a picture-show. I went to a picture-show in Pittsburgh last summer and it was so cold I almost caught p-neumonia.'

'We got our own method of air-conditioning down here, Miss Catherine.'

'Is that a fact? How's your drink, James—is that a fact?'

'It sure is.'

'And what's that?

'I'll take a little more, honey. Oops! That's enough.'

'And what's that, Henry?'

'Strip poker.'

'Strip poker?'

'Yeah.'

'You ever play strip poker, honey?'

'I heard tell about it, but I ain't never played it.'

'Me and James will be glad to show you, Miss Catherine.'

'I'm sure you would.'

'Ain't nothing to it, honey. All you got to do is . . .'

'Yeah, and what happens after we strip?'

'Then you just let nature take its course.'

'Sure, honey. Ain't nothing to worry about.'

'James, you mean to tell me you'd make me undress in front of this strange man?'

'He ain't no stranger, honey. We been knowing one another for going on sixteen years. That right, Henry?'

'That's exactly right, my man.'

'I wouldn't give a damn ef you knowed him since Eartha Kitt was poor. *I* don't know him and I'm damned if I'm going lowrate myself in front of no stranger. Say. What you all up to, anyway?'

'We ain't up to nothing, honey.'

'Honest to God we ain't, Miss Catherine.'

'It ain't nothing but a simple little game.'

'Simple little game my left foot. You take your hands off'n me, Henry Taylor! What y'all take me for, noway, some kind of tramp? Both of y'all get on out'n here, 'fore I calls the *po*lice.'

'Calls the *po*lice . . .'

'You heard me.'

'Now come on, honey, you wouldn't do nothing like that, would you?'

'I wouldn't, huh? *Stop* it, James!'

'Wait a minute. Wait a minute, *wait* a minute. Ain't no need of us getting all excited just because I suggested a innocent little game. All we got to do is play it cool and think this thing out. That right, James?'

'I'm with you all the way, my man.'

'Yeah, I know them innocent little games.'

'Now come on, honey, don't act like that.'

'Ain't nothing to the game, Miss Catherine. If you win you don't have to take off a damn thing!'

'And if I lose?'

'Well then naturally . . .'

'Uh-huh. "Well then naturally." Playing against you all I'd have 'bout as much chance as a candied yam on Sunday. Y'all drink up and get on out'n here.'

'Now, honey, don't act like *that*.'

'Get on out'n here. Both of you.'

'Can I finish my beer?'

'Drink up and get OUT!'

'Will I see you tomorrow, honey?'

'You got a telescope?'

'Well, anyway, it was nice meeting you, Miss Catherine.'

'Sorry I can't say the same about you.'

'Night-night, honey. I'll call you tomorrow.'

'Mmm-hmph. Be sure you make it long distance. A *very* long distance.'

'After you, James.'

'After you, my man.'

Sk-LAM!

'Wow! She didn't have to slam it *that* hard.'

'Man, you sure did mess up.'

'*I* messed up . . . what you mean *I* messed up? It was your idea, wasn't it?'

'Ouch!'

'What's wrong now?'

'I almost broke my ankle on that damn step.'

'I told you about it when we was coming in.'

'You sure did mess up. What you got to do is con*vince* 'em.'

'We convinced her, alright.'

'Which way you going?'

'I reckon I'll go on home.'

'OK. Be seeing you.'

'See you, old man.'

BLUEPLATE SPECIAL

A white man can't eat much. I know what I'm talking about, because I waited on nothing but white people for one whole summer in New York; or almost one whole summer, but we'll get to that. It was in a big restaurant in Sheepshead Bay, in Brooklyn, and there was about a hundred coloured employees including the chefs.

That was a real easy summer. It was in 1943, and most of the able-bodied men in the country had done been drafted. Back in them days a man with any sense at all—like me could make hisself a pile of money with no trouble and less effort. I was about to be drafted into the Army of the United States (to this day a lot of people don't know that it is an impossibility for any American of whatever race, creed or colour to be drafted into the United States Army) so I was just biding my time. I was real spry in them days, before the Army gave me bad feet, and because of the manpower situation I told y'all about I had what they call a free hand.

I was working three tables for two—'three deuces'—just by the east entrance to the joint, and it was one of the

129

best stations in the house. You never had to work hard, and yet your turnover was so fast that you made yourself a pile. If I didn't come away from that place with fifteen bucks on any given night of God's week I had the *blues*, pops, something terrible. While the other kats was crying about no business and yelling their heads off trying to get a party to sit at their tables I *always* had me a cool couple scarfing up a little storm and another couple mooing and wooing. I had it made. And then all of a sudden, BLAM! The Captain of the waiters comes up to me one afternoon and says, 'Look-a-here, Jones, I'm sorry, daddy, but I got to change your station. You see, it's like this . . .'

'Aw, maaaaan,' I says, 'don't be laying that jive on me. *You* know better than that.'

'No, no, man, dig!' he says.

'*Tsk*! . . . Man, I'll go out and get myself a defence job,' I says. '*I* don't have to work here.'

'Don't jump salty, Jones, dig what I'm 'bout to put down! Damn, man, you won't even let a man speak!'

'Fairy tales, man,' I says. 'Go tell it to them other kats.'

You dig, I could talk to the Captain like that because of this here manpower shortage. But I couldn't hype him. He was a hipster from WAY back. Real smooth kat that looked like a Mexican, and drove a Cadillac. If he didn't pull down three Cs a week he was MOST unhappy. So he says, 'Come on,' and I follow him on back, way way on back to the back of the place. Meanwhile he's laying a hype on me so thick you couldn't dent it with an electric drill:

'Ain't nothing to it, Jones, all you gotta do is be cool. The loot you'll make here will make them three deuces look like chicken feed, man, I'm here to tell you. I used to work this station myself before I became Captain and all you gotta do is see that these ofays don't run all over you.'

'Uh-huh,' I says.

'Just be cool, man, that's all. Don't take no shit from nobody because that ain't what you're here for, you dig? Just lay the food on them real nice and easy and if anybody gives you a hard time just come and see me, y'understand? Then everything will be cosy.'

'Crazy,' I says.

'Solid?'

'Solid.'

I didn't *have* to do it, you see, but in the meantime he'd done laid a sob story on me about five waiters being drafted the week before and two men leaving this week, so I figured I'd do my bit for the country even *before* I got in uniform, you dig? Wow, man, what a fool I was. Look what happened:

I stood there for an hour: nothing shaking. Two hours. Nothing. *Three* hours. About this time I'm picking up on this Captain kat, you dig? What is this stud putting down? War or *no* war, you dig? Where does this stud get so *strong*? Well, I'm *real* salty now. I count the money I have in my pocket and find that I have seven bucks. So I go downstairs to the locker room, get in a crap game to try to increase it a little bit and three passes later there I am with a buck seventy-five. So I go on back to my station.

What the hell is *this*, man, y'understand? And meantime . . . meantime all them other stations is *jumping*, pops! Niggers is making theyselves all *kinds* of loot and there I am with nothing but the tablecloths and menus. About that time I started thinking about *Defence*, man!

US Steel, US Rubber, Fairchild, all them *big* companies paying all that loot and there I am stuck in the suburbs of Brooklyn with a buck seventy-five. Sheeeeit, man, you dig? I was about to pack up and head for home when I heard what sounded like a ARMY coming down the aisle. I got right happy: got to straightening out the tablecloths, wiping off the knives and forks that had little water-spots on them and things like that—then I turned around and counted heads. One, two, four, eight, ten, fourteen. Jesus H. Christ. All I wanted was *four*! A small party that wouldn't give me a hard time and leave at least a fin, y'understand? Three like that and I'd have it made. But no. FOURTEEN!

And you shoulda seen them. You talk about hillbilly squares? Man, you ain't *seen* no squares till you see the Brooklyn variety: loud, open-neck sport shirts, light blue garbardine slacks, hairy chests—the works. Anyway I kept my cool. I showed my pearly whites, pulled the tables together right quick so that they made one big table, helped seat the chicks, and passed out the menus. Then I stood back and looked at them. Whew! What a crew! John Huston woulda been happy out of his *head* with a cast like that.

Well, the thing that you do in a situation like that is that you figure out who the Chief Stud is. So I cased the crowd and decided that this kat at the head of the table was The Man. Great big overgrown kat, he was, that looked like Bela Lugosi. I go up to him with pad in hand and say, in my best Virginia accent, 'Can I help you, suh?'

'Uh . . .' he says. I keep bending over close to him with my pad in my hand, but when he doesn't say anything I dig that I might be bugging him or something so I drop my hands and stand back.

'Whaddya want, honey?' he says to the chick on his left. She had a handkerchief to her nose, and was real busy with it.

'Aounowatiwan,' she says.

'Come again?' the Chief Stud says.

'I said I dunno what I want. Whatsa matter, can't ya *hear*?'

After the chick came on so strong the Chief Stud copped a plea: 'Whyn't ya have a steak, honey?' he says. But the chick iggs him completely. He goes back to his menu looking like he'd been beat over the head with something. Then all of a sudden all hell breaks loose:

'Steak, rare.'

'Steak, well done.'

'Broiled lobster.'

'Steamed clams.'

'Blueplate Special.'

'Cherrystone clams.'

'Clam bisque.'

'Make that two rare steaks.'

'Clam stew.'

'Lobster *au gratin*.'

'Make that two steamed clams.'

'Make that four rare steaks.'

'Hold it, I says. 'Hold it, hold it, HOLD IT . . . ladies and gentlemen. What would you like with that rare steak, sir?'

'Me? I didn't order no rare steak. I ordered a well-done steak.'

'Very well, sir. What would you like with it?'

'What you got?'

'Well, we have stringbeans, peas, cauliflower, corn-on-the-cob, mashed potatoes, julienne potatoes, carrots . . .'

'Anything else?'

'Er . . . lettuce . . .'

'I'll take lettuce. And mashed potatoes. Lots of it.'

'Very well, sir. And what would you like with that rare steak, ma'am?'

'What you got?'

'Well, we have stringbeans, peas, cauliflower, corn-on-the-cob, mashed potatoes, julienne potatoes, carrots, lettuce . . .'

'You got sweet potatoes?'

'No, ma'am.'

'Awright, gimme mashed. And carrots.'

'Yes, ma'am. And what would you like after those cherrystone clams, ma'am?'

'I'll take a broiled halibut.'

'Very good. And what would you like with it?'

'Stringbeans and julienne potatoes.'

'Very well, ma'am. And what was your order, sir?'

'Uh . . .'

'Come on, Bugsy,' the Chief Stud says, 'have a steak.'

'Aaaaaanh!' Bugsy says.

'Come on, Bugsy, be a sport.'

'Aaaaaanh!'

'Yeah, Bugsy,' Blownose says. 'Give you blood!'

'Awright, waiter,' Bugsy says. 'Gimme a steak, too.'

'Attaboy, Bugsy!'

'And what will you have with it, sir?'

'What you got?'

'Well, we have stringbeans, peas, cauliflower, corn-on-the-cob, mashed potatoes, julienne potatoes, carrots . . . lettuce . . .'

'You ain't got sweet potatoes, huh?'

'No, sir.'

'Awright, gimme mashed.'

'Attaboy, Bugsy!'

'Anything else, sir?'

'Yeah, peas.'

'Very well, sir. And you?'

'Me?'

'Yes, sir?'

'What about me?'

'You ordered steamed clams, didn't you?'

'Sure I ordered steamed clams.'

'Would you like anything after them?'

'Oh! Oh, yeah, uh . . . tell me what's *good*, waiter.'

'The steaks are excellent, sir.'

'You sure? You wouldn't kid me, would you?'

'No, I sure wouldn't.'

'OK, gimme a steak, too.'

'Very well, sir. And what would you like with it?'

'What you got?'

Wow, man, wow! I had to go through the whole stringbean bit all over again, you dig? And it went on like that for half an hour, man, I swear! I admire them other waiters for being able to put up with it, but I couldn't quite make it. So I went downstairs to the locker room, changed into my street clothes, walked outside and caught the Seabreeze Special back to New York. To hell with it, man, you dig? I went up to Harlem and got high, and for the rest of the summer I laid up in bed and played crazy. Then I got drafted.

But I still say a white man can't eat much. I watched them for almost a whole summer, so I know what I'm talking about.

COMRADE

Even now when I think of a German I think of him as a
'Comrade'. This is because by the time my outfit got to
Würzburg in the spring of 1945 nearbout every German
we seen was shouting '*Kamerad!*'; and for a long time we
thought they was saying 'Comrade', till our platoon leader—
a white-haired 1st Lieutenant from Sioux Falls, North
Dakota, named Lieutenant Dodkins—told us different.
But even after that a German to us was a Comrade.

I was in a Quartermaster outfit at the time, and we was
bivouacked a little ways outside the town near a place they
call the Flak Kaserne. A German anti-aircraft battalion used
to be in the Flak Kaserne, and now they were looking for
booby-traps before our outfit moved in it. There was three
barracks to it. They was long, low buildings with brown and
green and black paint on the sides of them. Sometimes when
I looked at the one that was facing our tents I thought I
could see a man running 'longside of it, but then I'd look
again and I'd see it was the crazy pattern the paint made.

The fighting had done moved ahead of us, and the
rumour was that we was supposed to be stationed in

Würzburg as part of a supply depot. Excepting booby-traps there won't nothing to worry about. Day and night you could hear planes going overhead so that most times the other person had to shout before you could hear him, but that was all.

It was a week before we moved in the Kaserne, but what I'm about to tell you happened the night after we got to Würzburg. I had guard duty that night. I was stationed outside a small square building that had a power station inside it. Leastways I thought it was a power station. There was a hum inside it like an electric generator was working. When the OG was gone I tried to open the door to look inside it, but it was locked. The OG is the Officer of the Guard.

The war had done moved on, like I said, so we all relaxed a little. When the OG was outa sight I set down and leaned my M-1 against the wall and lit a cigarette, cupping my hand over the flame. I thought of taking my helmet off—it was heavy and I never got used to the fact that it make your head waggle after you worn it a while—but I thought I better not. Instead I leaned my head back and tilted the helmet back a little, and when I did it made a scraping sound against the brick wall. I was tired. We'd been loading ammunition on to trucks most o' the day, and my back was sore. There was a moon out that night, and some town way in the distant was being bombed. You could just barely hear it. It sounded something like somebody bumping a trunk down the stairs in the next building. From the angle I was setting at it looked like somebody was trying to light matches to the moon. Then this stopped, and there was nothing but the steady flame and the sound of planes like bass violins being tuned.

I felt sleepy. I remembered the Article of War we was taught back in basic training about sleeping on guard duty, so I got up and paced back and forth a while in the military manner. Then it occurred to me that I could hear the OG coming long before he could see me, so I said to hell with it and set down again.

At first I thought it was him that woke me. I almost jumped outa my skin. I grabbed my rifle right quick, from reflex, and looked around. There was nobody in sight. But I was wide awake now. I listened real good, and when I didn't hear any footsteps I leaned back against the wall, slow-like. Then I heard the sound again. My hands was gripping the M-1 real tight, and I could feel my palms beginning to sweat. I thought of challenging, but I figured if that was a Comrade it might be my last challenge, so I kept my mouth shut.

There was a clump of bushes twenty or thirty yards from where I was sitting, and that was where the sound was coming from. The OG and me had done looked the area over real good, so I couldn't figure out how who—or whatever it was could be there. I sure'n hell didn't sleep *that* long, I thought. And there it was again. Well, Comrade, I thought, either you or me ain't goin' see our *Chatze* any more, and I'm goin' make damn sure it's *you*.

I eased down flat on my stomach, with my left elbow well in front for a good steady prop and my trigger hand close to my nose, and took a bead on the bush. I was getting trigger-happy. I wanted to shoot into the bush then maybe I'd see him and finish him. I was still thinking this over when I seen what it was: a dog.

A big dog. German police. He was creeping up to me real slow. I was about to shoot it when I seen it was dragging its hind legs. I got up. When I did he seen me and growled; a real low, mean growl.

'*Come* 'ere, boy!' I said. He got to growlin' again, real low in his throat. I snapped my fingers. '*Come* 'ere, boy!' He lay still and looked at me, snarling. I had two cans of 'C' rations in my pack, so I leaned my rifle against the wall and took out one of them and got to opening it. He was laying there looking at me all the time, his eyes bright and yellow like a cat's. When I got the lid off I shook the stuff out—it was cold so it came out solid—and threw it to him. He jumped back and snarled, looking at me with his teeth bared. 'You big bastard,' I said out loud, 'if you try to bite me I'll blow your head off.' I reached and got my rifle and stood there lookin' down at him. After a time he got to sniffing around. He'd stop and growl every time I made a move. I just stood there, with the rifle pointed at his head. That dog musta sniffed at that food a good fifteen minutes before he would touch it. Then he et it in about three bites, and looked up at me.

'Come 'ere, boy! *Come* on! . . .' I whistled at him. I stooped down and opened the other can and threw it to him. He jumped back again, but this time he ate it after only a few sniffs.

'*Come* on, boy!'

He got to inchin' up to me real slow, draggin' his hind legs. He made like to get up, but he couldn't make it so he lay down again. The fire from the town that was bombed way in the distant was dying down, and the planes was gone. It was quiet now, and when I stood up I could hear my boots scrape against the gravel. I thought of going to the dog, but I figured it would be better if he came to me. I kept snappin' my fingers and calling him, and he kept comin' closer. I could see his head clear, now: big and shaggy and evil-looking; but he won't growling no more. When he was a few feet from me I reached out my hand. He growled and moved back. I had my rifle on my lap, and it hit me that that might be what he was afraid of. So I set it down on the ground and reached out my hand again.

'*Come* on, boy!'

He inched up closer and closer, sniffing my hand. When I touched his head he flinched, but didn't make a sound. I stroked his head and got to talkin' to him real soft. 'I'm Frank DeVoe,' I said. 'I'm an American soldier. I know you was brought up not to like American soldiers, and frankly I don t give much of a damn about you, either, but if you behave yourself I'll get them legs o' yours fixed up so's you can walk. You goin' be nice?'

The crazy dog got to growlin' again, but I kept on strokin' his head. Then he turned, right sudden-like, and barked. The OG was coming round the side of the building.

'Easy boy,' I said. 'Easy now.' I stood up and saluted.

'What the devil've you got there, DeVoe?'

'A dog, sir.'

'Where the hell'd you get 'im?'

'I didn't, sir. He come up to me.'

'Just like that, huh? Well, get rid of 'im. Everything else alright?'

'Yes, sir.'

'Your relief will be here in half an hour. Get rid of that hound.'

'Yes, sir.'

He returned my salute and walked away. When he was gone I knelt down again and patted the dog's head. He won't ornery no more, but I could tell he was still tense. 'Let's see your legs, big boy,' I said. I set down my rifle and picked up one of his hind legs. He growled. I told him to shut up and looked at the leg. It had a long gash in it, but in the half-light I couldn't tell if it was a knife wound or what. His other leg was cut, too, but not as bad. 'You sure got yourself in a fix, boy,' I said. I stood up.

I got to thinking of what to do. I could take him to the medic's tent and get Blackie Brown to fix him up. Blackie would do it. But then what? I couldn't hardly keep him, even if I wanted to. And I wasn't sure I wanted to.

When I got to the medic's tent, with all nine thousand pounds of dog across my shoulder, Blackie Brown was sitting on a folding chair with his feet up on a table reading a magazine.

'Evenin', Corporal!' I said, and set the dog down on the ground. Blackie turned around.

'What in the hell have *you* got?' he said. 'Git that damn dog out'n my tent.'

'He's hurt, Blackie. I want you to fix him up.'

'You ignorant black bastard, *git* that damn Kraut dog out'n my tent.'

'Fix the damn dog up, Blackie, and quit bein' evil.'

''Fore I touch 'im Betty Grable'll turn blacker'n the ace o' spades,' Blackie said, but he was bending over the dog. The dog growled.

'Easy, boy,' I said. 'You'll be OK in a minute.'

'Ain't nothin I kin do but clean the wounds out and bandage them,' Blackie said, 'then I hope the son of a bitch drops dead.'

I held the dog's head and talked to him while Blackie washed the wounds and dressed them. It musta hurt, but he didn't utter nary a sound. I took and got some water in a basin and gave it to him. He lapped it up and I give some more. Blackie had done set down with his magazine again, just like we won't there.

'How you feel, boy? Feel better now?'

'Git that dog out'n my tent, DeVoe.'

'Feel better, boy? Hunh?' I rubbed the dog's head.

'DeVoe, if you don't get that dog out'n here I'll shoot you, so help me God. And your mother won't collect no insurance, neither.'

'You nappy-head bastard,' I said, 'I bet if it was a woman you wouldn't talk like that.' Blackie laughed.

'Come on, boy! Get up, boy!' I said. The dog got to his feet, real slow. He could barely walk, but he was waggin' his tail like all get out.

'Now git outa here, both of you,' Blackie said. I picked up my rifle and walked out the tent with the dog limpin' along behind me.

Even before we got to the Kaserne there won't no question about the dog staying with me. He just wouldn't leave. And if anybody but me much as came near him he'd growl so fierce that they let him alone. He was mine. Only it look to me sometimes like I was his. He'd lay down by my cot, and after we got to the Kaserne he'd lay down by my bunk. When I got up *he'd* get up. If I went out on a detail you could bet your case ace he'd be there too, watchin' me work. I called him Fritz.

One day I was walkin' through the town—or rather what was left of the town, 'cause there won't much to it but piles of rubble—with Fritz trotting along behind me. He was well now, though you could still see the scars. I was on my way to a little *Gasthaus* that had done opened up. It was the first one to open up after we got to Würzburg.

I was nearbout to the place, picking my way through the loose bricks and holes, when I seen a girl coming from the other direction, picking her way along just like I was. When she got close to me she seen the dog and stopped.

'*Ach, du lieber Gott*,' she said, 'Caesar!' Only she didn't say it like that. She said 'Tsayzar'. The dog got to waggin' his tail, but he wouldn't go to her.

'*Ach, du liebes Kind*,' she said, and put her arms around the dog. Fritz didn't look overjoyed to see her, but I figured he probably belonged to her friends or family because he let her pet him.

'This your dog?' I said.

'*Wie, bitte?*'

'This,' I pointed to the dog and then to her, 'yours?'

'*Ja!*' she said. She was nodding her head like crazy, and smiling. She had a navy blue shawl over her head and a blue overcoat with shoulders on it like you see on German uniforms. She was fifteen, maybe sixteen.

'Take 'im,' I said. 'Go on home, Fritz!' But Fritz wouldn't move. He just stood there waggin' his tail, with his tongue out, lookin' at me. 'Go on home, boy!'

The girl said something in German that I didn't understand. I said goodbye to her and to Fritz and went inside the *Gasthaus.* I wasn't in there five minutes before Fritz come in, pushin' the door open just like a man and coming in and laying down by my table. 'I'll be damn,' I said. 'I'll just be damn.'

That night it was all over the barracks. After lights out everybody got on me.

'That nigger ain't after Comrade's dogs,' somebody said. 'He's after Comrade's daughters.' They all laughed.

'Yeah, I know Frank DeVoe from *way* back. That nigger'll rob a cradle in a minute.'

'Old Frank DeVoe's a *lover*, that's what *he* is.'

'What you goin' do now, Lover DeVoe?'

'I know what he *better* do. He better leave Comrade's dogs *and* Comrade's daughters alone, 'cause Comrade is a BAD number.' They all laughed again.

The next day I was in a poker game with a few of the boys—it was a Saturday—when a messenger come in from the orderly room. I was holdin' a pair o' queens with one in the hole when he come up to me and said, 'You got a guest, DeVoe.'

'Hold it a minute,' I said. 'Deal 'em.'

'You better come right now.'

'Deal 'em, man.'

'Lieutenant Dodkins said for you to—'

'Deal the cards.'

I lost the hand anyway, to two pairs. When I got to the orderly room there was a German standing there, a man in his late fifties with hair like you see on classical musicians. I coulda sworn he was wearing the same coat I seen on the girl the day before. He was a little man with bright blue eyes.

'DeVoe, this is Herr Schaub,' Lieutenant Dodkins said, 'and he says you have his dog.' Herr Schaub was smiling and nodding in that stiff way Comrade has.

'I tried to give it back yesterday,' I said. 'Was that your daughter?'

'Please?'

'I said was that your daughter I met yesterday?'

'Yess, yess!' Herr Schaub said, and nodded again. His teeth was yellow, but somehow it made his face look pleasant.

'Where's the dog now?' Lieutenant Dodkins said.

'He's probably right outside,' I said.

'Bring him in.'

The orderly opened the door and the dog came in, wagging his tail. Herr Schaub made a lot of fuss over him, but he didn't act like Herr Schaub was his best friend. He lowered his head and let Herr Schaub pat him, then he looked up at me and got to waggin' his tail again.

'I can take him now, yes?' Herr Schaub said.

'He's all yours,' Lieutenant Dodkins said.

'Sure,' I said. 'Go on home, Fritz.' I patted his head. 'Go home like a good boy.'

We all went outside and stood in the courtyard. In the sunlight Herr Schaub looked smaller than he did in the orderly room, and his shoulders was stooped. He lifted his hat and smiled at all of us and said '*Vielert Dank*!' then put on his hat again and started down the driveway. Fritz started after him, then stopped and looked around at me. Herr Schaub stopped and turned around too. He called the dog, but the dog wouldn't move. He called him again. Herr Schaub came back to us and said, 'That is very strange.' He said 'tsat' instead of 'that', and he pronounced his *R*s way back in his throat. He turned to me and said, '*Vielleicht* . . . perhaps if you will come with me he will go home, yes?'

I turned to Lieutenant Dodkins. 'Go ahead,' he said. I went to the barracks and put on a tie and changed from my fatigues to a field jacket and OD trousers and strapped on my pistol belt and came back outside. Fritz was standing by Herr Schaub, but he was looking at the barracks door when I came out. Herr Schaub and I started down the driveway, with the dog walking on my side.

'You can't hardly talk good English, can you?' I said.

'Please?'

'I said your English ain't so hot.'

'Hot?'

'Yeah, good. Your English no good.'

'Oh. It has been a long time.'

'Where'd you pick it up?'

'Please?'

'Where did you learn English?'

'It has been a long time. In the gymnasium.'

'In a gymnasium?'

'Yes. How do you say . . . *High* School.' He looked real proud of hisself.

'Was you in the Army?'

'Ach! . . . No, no. I am too old for tsat.'

'Say "that".'

'Tsat.'

'*That. Thhh! Thhhh!*'

'*Sssss! Sssss!*'

We'd done stopped in the middle of the driveway, and we both laughed. We could tell we liked one another, and it was a nice feelin'.

'Where do you live in America?'

'I'm from Alabama.'

'Ach, so. Alabama. I do not know Alabama.'

'You been to the States?'

'Please?'

'*You* know . . . America. You been to America?'

'Ach, so! Yes, yes I have been to America.'

'When was you there?'

'It has been a long time. I was in New York.'

'You get up to Harlem?'

'Please?'

'I say did you make Harlem? *You* know. *Harlem.*'

'Ah! *Haaar*lem! No, no, no, I did not.'

'You oughta make it. It swings.'

'Please?'

'I said Harlem *swings. You* know . . . dat-tee-dat-dat-dadat-taa! Like that.'

We both laughed again. He had a way of shaking his head from side to side when he said 'No', like he was shuddering; and when he said 'Please?' he would stop and put a hand to his ear and his eyes would light up, real blue. We looked at each other and laughed again, for no good reason at all, and walked on.

The main road through town was mostly cleared of rubble by now. The bricks were piled up to the level of bombed-out windows, and on top of one big pile there was some kids playing. From way up north there was the sound of bombs or heavy artillery. I couldn't tell which at first, then I recognized it was big guns. I wondered how Herr Schaub felt about it. I looked at him, but there won't much of an expression on his face. He was walking with his shoulders hunched over and his head down, and every once in a while he would sniff real loud and clear his throat. I thought to ask him how the dog had got wounded, but I decided to let him tell it if he felt like it.

'Do you know German?'

'Jus' a little,' I said. 'I picked up a little from a book they give us back in France.'

'Ah, yes. France. Did you learn any French?'

'Only one sentence. *Voulez-vous . . .*'

'Yes, yes, yes,' he said right fast, 'I know that one, too.' He looked kinda embarrassed, but he smiled at me.

When we got to what musta been the nine hundredth pile of rubble Herr Schaub stopped and took off his hat. He held it at his side a minute and then put it on again and said 'This way, please.' I followed him around the back through a little path and there was part of a two-story brick house still standing. The windows was out and the blast marks on the side of it made it look as if it had a giant case of smallpox, but it looked pretty good compared to the rest of the houses in the town. Inside the ground floor room there was signs of plaster dust in the corners, but other than that it was clean and smelled cool like fresh cement. I could see they had salvaged what they could from the front of the house and put it in this room. There was books and pictures and linen piled everywheres.

'Anna!' Herr Schaub called out. '*Ich habe einen Neger mit mir!*'

'You say that again and I'll punch you in the mouth,' I said.

'Please?'

'You heard me.'

'Please excuse me. I do not understand.' His face was real serious now, and his eyes looked then like I know now they had looked for a long time: real sad.

'Don't say that no more,' I said. He threw up his hands and cried out like somebody had done hit him; then he set down to a table and pushed some linen away with his elbows and leaned his head in his hands. He shook his head from side to side.

'*Nein, nein, nein, nein, nein*,' he said, still shaking his head. 'You do not . . . you have not . . . you have misunderstood.' He got up then and walked around a little with his hand to his chin, like he was thinking. Then he said, 'Do you know Latin?'

'No.'

'Then please listen. The Latin word for "black" is *niger*. The German word for "a blackman" is *Neger*, but it derives from the Latin word. Do you understand? I did not mean to-to-to . . .'

'I understand,' I said. I felt right foolish. A woman came down the stairs just then; a plump woman with blonde hair and a round face with fine veins showing through her skin.

'I am sorry but I do not know your name,' Herr Schaub said to me. His eyes was still sad.

'DeVoe,' I said. 'PFC DeVoe.'

'My wife, Frau Schaub.'

'*Guten Tag*,' she said, and offered her hand.

'Glad to meet you.'

'*Er hat unseren Hund mitgebracht,*' Herr Schaub said. Then he said something else I didn't catch. Frau Schaub went over to the dog and petted him. He didn't get up, but wagged his tail. Frau Schaub noticed the scars, and said something to Herr Schaub I didn't understand.

'I guess I better be gettin' back,' I said.

'Please?'

'I got to get back to the Kaserne.'

'Ah, yes. Can you not stay for a moment?'

'I reckon I can. But not for long.'

'Sit down, please,' Herr Schaub said. He brought me a chair.

'How did . . . was he hurt?' He pointed to the dog. I told him what happened, but not all. I didn't tell him I almost shot the dog, and I told him it was me that bandaged him. When I got through he said it to Frau Schaub in German, and they both thanked me.

'Please, will you have some coffee? I have also a little *Weinbrand*. The coffee is not real coffee, but the *Weinbrand* is good.' He was smiling now.

'I'll take some o' that *Weinbrand*,' I said.

When we had done toasted one another—with Herr Schaub holding his glass up and looking in my eyes then taking a sip and holding it up like that again—we got to talking. He told me he used to be a professor of philology at the University of Darmstadt, and when I asked him what philology was he explained it to me. The daughter came in while we was talking and said *Guten Tag* and petted the dog (she curtsied when she said *Guten Tag* and it kinda tickled me, but I liked it), then she and the mother went upstairs. Herr Schaub told me that the German outfit that was in the Kaserne before us had taken the dog away from him about a year ago, and he hadn't seen him since. He thought the dog was dead.

When I got up to leave Frau Schaub and the daughter came downstairs and we all shook hands, then Herr Schaub walked outside with me.

'There is one thing I must tell you,' he said as we walked back to the street. I didn't have no idea what that could be, but I sure didn't expect what was coming. 'The word your people do not like,' he said, '. . . you know the one I . . . I refer to?'

'Yeah, I know.'

'Well, then. That word is a . . . a Cockney mispronunciation of the German word *Neger* on the part of English sailors in the seventeenth century.' He shook his head from side to side like he was impatient and said, '*Tsk!* Simply a Cockney mispronunciation. So you should not . . . you *must* not be offended even when *that* word is used. Do you understand?'

'I'll think about it,' I said.

'Well, then. Goodbye and thank you again.'

'Goodbye, sir.'

Our outfit moved up to Frankfurt the next week, so I never saw him or the dog again. But if Herr Schaub ever reads this I'd like him to know that Comrade is OK by me, and I hope we never have to fight one another no more.

DANCE OF THE INFIDELS

I used to listen to jazz all day and most the night. I'd go to bed by it and wake up with it. Look like nobody else in town was as crazy about it as me; they all said I was 'music happy'. But that was OK by me. They live their life and I live my own.

I used to go to a little café on Davis Street a whole lot. There was a big old jukebox in the place, and I'd stoop over and put my ear right up against the speaker and listen. That way all I could hear in the whole wide world was music, and that was fine with me. So this night when I walked in the café and seen a man doing the same thing—leaning down with his ear against the speaker—I went over and tapped him on the shoulder.

He looked up. I hadn't never seen him before. 'I got that record at home,' I said.

'Oh, yeah?'

'Yeah.'

'Well that's crazy,' he said, and put his ear to the speaker again. Even while he was stooped over I could tell he was taller than me. When the record was finished and he stood up I noticed that his eyes had a real far-away look in them, like he was used to looking at mountains from a distance.

'You want to go over to my place and listen to records?' I said. He just looked at me, real blank. Then he said 'Crazy,' and we went outside to the street. He walked like he had springs in the toes of his shoes; like every step he took was going to be a long one, so that you were always surprised at how short they were. All the way to my place he didn't say a word. Most times we walked with enough room between us for a growed woman to walk through. Then one time a man passed us and we had to move together to let him by. Our coat sleeves touched, and he jumped like he'd been burnt. 'What the hell is this?' I thought to myself. I got to thinking right then of how to get rid of him without hurting his feelings.

When we got to my place I offered him a seat, but he didn't sit down. I don't mean to say nothing derogatory about him, but he acted just like a dog acts when he gets to a place he ain't never been in before: he walked all around and sniffed at things. You could almost hear him sniffing out loud.

'You want a drink?' I said.

'You got wine?'

'I ain't got nothing but whisky.'

'No thanks.'

'I can go get some wine, if you want.'

'I'll go get it,' he said.

'No, I'll get it. Make yourself at home.'

I went out and got the wine and when I got back he was sitting in a chair with his legs crossed. I still couldn't figure him out. He looked like he was in a world all his own.

'You blow?' he said.

'Blow?'

'Yeah. You play anything?'

'No. No, I don't play nothing. You?'

'I blow box.'

'You blow what?'

'Piano.'

He sounded irritant because I couldn't understand everything he said.

'You from around here?'

'I'm from The Apple,' he said. Then he knew right off I didn't get it so he said, 'New York. I'm down here visiting my people.'

I poured myself a drink and turned on the record player. Then I remembered that I hadn't opened the wine bottle, so I opened it and poured him a drink. While the record player was warming up I got to leafing through the records. He came over and stood beside me, so I held the records so's he could read the labels. Our coat sleeves touched again and he moved away a little. I handed the records to him and said, 'Here. Why'nt you play what you want?' I said it real soft so's not to offend him and went over and sat on the couch.

He got to looking through the records, and every once in a while he'd say, 'Solid!' Then he got to laughing. Not at me or anything in particular; just laughing.

'Where'd you pick up on these, man?'

'I gets them from a store in New York,' I said. I meant to say The Apple instead of New York, and I was sorry I didn't. He turned around and looked at me, half-smiling, like *he* was the one that was trying to figure *me* out.

He put a record on the player. It was 'Salt Peanuts' by Dizzie Gillespie, with Don Byas on tenor sax. I thought to tell him that that was the first one I bought, that I got it while I was in the Army in New Orleans; but I didn't. He turned the volume up real loud and sat down. I got up and turned it down a little. I knew he'd be disappointed so I said, 'Neighbours.' He nodded.

We sat there listening for a while, neither of us talking. Then he got to riffing Dizzie's solo out loud. 'Well I'll be damn!' I thought. I knew the solo real well myself, so I riffed right along with him. I kept listening for him to make a mistake. He didn't. When the solo was over we looked at one another, both of us smiling. It was like looking at somebody and thinking for a split minute that you was looking at yourself. We both laughed. He got up and came over to me and stretched his hand out.

'Skin,' he said. I slapped his palm real light and he said, 'Solid.' Then we shook hands, and he sat down again. I felt a lot better about his being there. In fact, I felt right then that he could stay there for the rest of his natural life, Amen.

We sat there for about an hour, riffing and listening: Bird, Miles Davis, Dizzie, Bud Powell . . . strictly the kick. He was mostly playing records with Bud on them, so he could listen to the piano. We was having a natural ball.

Then he turned to me and said, 'Do you turn?'

'Do I what?'

'Aw, man,' he said. He looked real disgusted. I'd heard what he said, alright, but I had to have time to figure out what he meant. Then I got it.

'You mean do I smoke?'

'Yeah, man. Yeah.'

'No,' I said, 'but you can go 'head if you want.'

I hadn't never seen anybody smoke marijuana. I'd heard it was bad, so I stayed away from it. But I figured that if he wanted to do it that was his business, not mine. I poured myself another drink and sipped it. He didn't move. When the record was over I got up and took it off. 'What you wanna hear?' I said.

'Play some J. J.,' he said. His mood had done changed, and mine had, too. 'God damn pot head,' I thought. But I liked him—after all, he was the first person I'd met who loved jazz as much as I do—so I was sorry I'd thought it. I found a record by J. J. Johnson and put it on. He still didn't move, just sat there looking down at the floor, like he was thinking. Then he cursed—real soft, but I heard it—and reached in his coat pocket and took out a reefer. He straightened out the ends of it and lit it.

I sat there watching him smoke—taking deep drags and then holding his breath so that no smoke came out—and I thought: what the hell; once won't hurt, will it?

'Gimme a drag,' I said. He handed it to me without a word and I took it. I smoked it just like he had, holding my breath so that the smoke stayed down. We both smoked it, passing it back and forth till it was down to a fraction. Then he put it out and put it in his pocket. 'Gotta save roaches,' he said, and smiled.

For a while I didn't feel anything; just the whisky. Then I got up to change the record—that is I started getting up, because it looked like I'd never stop rising up off that couch—and I knew it had hit me. I took the record off and put on 'Scrapple from the Apple' by Charlie Parker, then sat back down. While I was doing it I noticed that everything in the room looked like it had shifted just a little bit; like somebody had come in and moved everything a little up and to the left.

But it was sitting there listening to Bird and Miles playing in unison that I really got the feel of it. I got up and turned the volume up a little, then sat back down. I got up and turned it up some more. It was just like I'd heard them for the first time. I mean *really* heard them. I turned the record player up full blast. Wail, Bird. I tried to turn it up some more, but the damn thing just wouldn't go any louder. Wail, Bird. To hell with neighbours. To hell with everybody. WAIL, Bird!

We sat there and smoked a couple more sticks and got high as kites. After that he took to coming by my place nearbout every night, and when he ran out of pot it didn't matter. We'd get juiced and have ourselves an A-grade ball, listening and riffing.

I liked the pot. I liked it a whole lot. When Ronnie—his name was Ronald Johnston—went back to New York he promised he'd write to me and send me some. Sure enough, about a week after he was gone here come a newspaper addressed to me, all rolled up. I unrolled it real slow, and there was a small package of pot pasted on the inside sheet. On the covering of the package he wrote one word: 'Wail.'

I didn't hear from him after that. I wrote to him and thanked him for the pot, and when he didn't answer I wrote again: nothing. So along about March of the next year I went on up to New York.

I got off the train at Pennsylvania Station and went outside to 34th Street and got a taxi. It was the first time I had ever been to New York. I told the driver where I wanted to go—it was a house on 127th Street near Lenox Avenue—and he took me through the city and through Central Park and then up to Harlem. I liked New York a lot, especially driving through the park. Harlem wasn't nothing like I thought it would be. I'd always imagined there would be lots of shambly houses and all that; but it was all built up, just like the rest of New York. And to this day I've never got over that.

So anyway, me and this taxi go on up to 127th Street and I pay the driver and start up the stairs. I'd checked my bag at the train station, so I didn't have anything to carry. The building was old and dirty and even in the daytime it was dark. I got to Ronnie's apartment and rang the bell. Nothing happened. Instead of ringing it again, like I thought of doing, I just stood there and waited. There was a circle in the upper half of the door, and after a while it looked like it moved, so I tried to look through it. I couldn't.

'What do you want?' a man's voice said.

'Do Ronald Johnston live here?'

'What you want?' the voice said again.

'Do Ronald Johnston—'

The door opened, and a man with hair that looked like it had been pasted down with axle grease poked his head out. He blinked his eyes and said, 'Who're you?'

'I'm Benevolence Delaney,' I said.

'You're *who*?'

I said it again. He kind of smirked and looked me up and down from head to shoes. Then he said, 'He's not here. If you want to see him you can . . .' He looked me up and down again. 'He's at the Y-Bar. You know where that is?'

'No?

He told me where it was and I found it. It was almost as dark inside it as it had been in the apartment building. I went to the bar and ordered a shot, then looked around. We saw each other at about the same time. He was at the far end of the bar. He got up off his stool real slow, looking like he didn't believe what his eyes was showing him.

"Well I'll be gaaat-dam,' he said. 'My boy.' We shook hands and looked at one another.

'How you doin'?' I said.

'Aw, man,' he said. He looked me up and down just like his friend had done back at the apartment. I got the feeling he was embarrassed to see me; like I was a third cousin that was born on the wrong side of the river.

'You look good,' I said; but he didn't. He'd lost weight, and his clothes hung on him most like they do on a hatrack. When he talked his eyes kept shifting all around, like any minute he expected somebody to try and hit him.

'Ain't nothing shaking, huss,' he said. 'Nothing but dues, you dig? Kats won't let a man live. I had a gig up at The Track for a while—house band, you dig?—then my habit got me and I had to split but I kicked it and got another gig up in the Bronx. But them square mother-hubbers drug me so terrible 1 had to put that down. West Indians, you dig? I dig what they're sayin', man, but I can't make that time. How *you* doing, man? When'd you fall in town?'

He was talking real fast and looking all around, like I said, and I didn't hardly understand what he was talking about. I asked him what 'The Track' was and he told me it was the nickname for the Savoy Ballroom; only this time he didn't get irritant when I asked him. He was glad to see me, and said it. I told him I'd just got into town and he said, 'You got a pad?'

'No.'

'You could stay at my pad, but I'm sharing it with a stud.'

'I saw him,' I said. 'I reckon I'll get me a room in a hotel.'

'Solid,' he said. 'Let's fall down to the Dewey Square Hotel and get you a pad.'

We walked across town and caught a 7th Avenue bus and went down to the Dewey Square Hotel. I registered and then we went to a little square right near 116th Street and sat on a bench and talked. I asked him if he'd gotten my letters and he said yes. I thanked him again for the pot and said, 'You know where I can get some?'

'Some pot?'

'Yeah.'

'Ain't much shaking. The Man done put the finger on the kats and everybody's layin' low. My boy got busted.'

I looked at him and shook my head. I couldn't hardly understand a word that man said; but I learned to figure it out. He thought for a while and then he said, 'Come on, let's split.' We got up and walked over to 116th Street and 8th Avenue and caught the subway. We rode up to 145th Street and got off and went to a poolroom near the corner.

The poolroom was way bigger than the one back home, with about twelve tables to it. It was packed full of niggers. I followed Ronnie on back to the back of the place, edging by people, and when he stopped I stopped, too. It looked like he got real innerested in one of the games. The man that was shooting was real good. It looked like he was going run 'em all the way, eight-ball and all. I figured that Ronnie and me would be up soon, and I was kinda looking forward to a game. I noticed that nobody in the place was looking at anybody else; just at the pool tables. Then the man that was shooting missed. He cursed and lit a cigarette and moved back to the wall. He was standing right alongside of Ronnie. I just barely seen it, I swear, I seen him slip a couple of reefers into Ronnie's hand and Ronnie slipped him some money. They didn't look at one another once the whole time, and not a word was said. Then Ronnie said 'Come on', and we edged our way out to the street.

'That was real cool,' I said.

'*Got* to be, man, he said. 'The Man done put niggers on the police force so they can put the finger on other niggers. And the squares are all happy out of their heads just because they got coloured cops. Ain't that a bitch?'

'Yeah,' I said.

'The only stripes I dig are *pin*stripes, man. I ain't got no eyes a-tall for them wide ones. Come on, let's fall down to my pad and get happy.'

We caught the 145th Street crosstown bus and rode over to 8th Avenue, and then we caught the 8th Avenue bus and went down to 127th Street and walked across town to his pad. His room-mate wasn't at home. It was the funniest apartment I'd ever seen. As you come in the door the first thing that hits you is a painting of Our Lord and Saviour Jesus Christ with a crown of thorns on His head. His face looked so sad it nearbout scared me. Underneath it there was a sofa with a leopard skin cover. There was a piano against the wall, and even looking at it you could tell the tone wouldn't be so hot; it was old. Through an open doorway you could see a stove with a pot on it.

'Siddown,' Ronnie said. I started to sit on the sofa, but that leopard skin was a little too much for me so I sat in an armchair with a faded green cover on it. I did my best not to look at that leopard skin.

Ronnie went into the kitchen and got to fumbling around. I looked around for something to pass the time and picked up a book. It was *Native Son* by Richard Wright. I read the first page of it and all of a sudden there was a wild sound above my head; a sound of trumpets. It made me jump, and when I looked up Ronnie was standing in the doorway laughing his head off.

'Wake up and live, Bennie!' he said. 'Things to *come*, man!'

I laughed and put the book down. Then I saw that Ronnie'd done had a speaker rigged up in the front room. The record player was in the kitchen. He came in and lit up a stick or 'a joint', like he said, and handed it to me. I took a few deep drags and handed it back to him, with the sound of trumpets like drumbeats in my ears.

'You short, black son of a bitch,' Ronnie said, and laughed. He was glad to see me alright. I could tell by his eyes.

So we sat there and got high and listened to records. Then he said his room-mate would be back soon, and since

I didn't want to see him I left. I went down to Pennsylvania Station and got my bag out of check, then went to the Dewey Square. It was good to be in New York, and to be high again. It was real good.

I didn't see him for about a week after that. I'd go up to his place—he didn't have a telephone—and either nobody was there or his greasy-head room-mate would tell me he didn't know where Ronnie was. I went to the Y-Bar several times, but I never saw him. So I got to looking around town on my own. I went down to Broadway a few times and looked at all the bright lights and the big Camel advertisement of a man with smoke-rings coming out his mouth. I took in a few movies, and it was sitting in a picture-show one night that I figured out where I might find him. The Dewey Square Hotel is on 117th Street, and right around the corner from it is a nightclub called 'Minton's Playhouse'. Ronnie showed it to me when he first brought me to the hotel. And so, when the movie was over, I went uptown.

My hunch paid off. Minton's was divided into two sections. There was a bar with a jukebox in it, just like a regular bar. Then there was a swinging door and when it swung open you could hear live music coming from the inside room. Ronnie wasn't in the bar so I started into the back room. Somebody told me at the door that I'd have to pay more for my drinks in the back, but I said I didn't care and went on in. There was a row of tables on each side of a long room, and near the bandstand there was a dance floor about the size of a big playpen. It was dark inside, but most of the people were wearing dark glasses. I didn't know any of the musicians that were playing, but they were good. I sat at a table and ordered a drink. I didn't recognize Ronnie at first, because I hadn't ever seen him in dark glasses. I picked up my drink and went over and sat beside him. While the band was playing we didn't talk. When they stopped he said, 'Kicks to see you, man.' We shook hands.

'Where you been?' I said.

'Aw, man. I been goofing.'

'Oh, yeah?'

'Yeah, man. Dues, you dig? Gotta pay 'em.'

'I been looking for you,' I said.

'I'm hip.'

The band started up again, so we stopped talking and listened. I noticed he was drinking a coke, and I touched him and asked him by signal if he wanted a drink. He frowned and shook his head. After a long while he turned to me and said, 'You got any bread?'

'I ain't got much,' I said. 'How much you need?'

'Three cents,' he said.

'Three *cents*?'

'Three bucks, man.'

'Oh,' I said. 'Sure, I got that much.' I started to reach for the money but he stopped me. 'Let's split,' he said. I paid the waiter and we went outdoors.

He called a cab and we drove about fifteen blocks uptown. We got out and went to a bar. He just stood inside the doorway and looked all around. He didn't see who or what it was he wanted, so we walked on to another bar. Same thing. We walked about two blocks and crossed the street: same thing. After about three more bars—I was getting kinda tired of this because I wanted a drink—he saw who it was he was looking for. You could tell it the minute he walked in the door. He looked like a great big heavy sack had just been lifted off his shoulders.

'Wait here a minute,' he said. To hell with that, I thought. I went to the bar and ordered a double. Ronnie'd done gone to a booth and was talking to a man in a leather jacket and sky-blue pants. They both got up after a time and Ronnie signalled to me—all he did was raise his head a little—so I finished the drink and all three of us went outside.

The other man walked just like Ronnie did: with that springy, bouncy step that looked like he was about to take off and fly. We walked on up the block—none of us saying a mumbling word—and around a corner and into a building.

We started up the stairs, me going last, and as we walked past the fifth floor I heard what I thought first was a pigeon cooing and next a baby crying. But it was neither a baby or a pigeon. It was a woman; and she wasn't crying. We walked up to the seventh floor and Ronnie and the man stopped. We was all standing on the stairs, Ronnie on top and then the man and then me. I thought they were going to somebody's apartment, because there was a door right behind Ronnie. But they weren't.

'You got the bread, Bennie?' Ronnie said.

'Oh!' I said. Then I remembered that I'd spent all the small bills I had. 'I ain't got nothing but a ten-spot,' I said.

'I ain't got change for that,' the man said.

'We can get change later,' Ronnie said. I gave the man the ten-spot.

Ronnie took off his jacket and hung it on the doorknob. Then he took off his belt and rolled up the shirtsleeve on his left arm. His skin was grey under the light. The man took a spoon and a little bottle of water out of his jacket pocket. The bottom of the spoon was black. Next he brought out a little brown packet from another pocket and tapped what looked like garlic salt into the spoon from the packet. Then he poured some of the water from the bottle into the spoon, crumpled the empty packet, threw it down the stairs and said, 'Gimme a match.' I lit a match and handed it to him. Ronnie had done wrapped his belt tight around his arm just above the elbow. He was flexing his arm back and forth, and the veins in his forearm were standing out like veins on a dead leaf. The man held the flame to the bottom of the spoon and moved it around so that it heated even. Then he threw the match away and took a hypodermic needle out of his jacket. He sucked all the melted liquid up with the needle, then handed it to Ronnie. Ronnie took it. You could hear him breathing hard. It looked as though he was looking for the right vein. He moved his arm around so that the light would hit it right, meanwhile flexing his fist. I heard the woman on the fifth floor half-shout and half-scream and call a man's name twice. Then her voice sounded like it was muffled in a pillow and the needle was in Ronnie's arm. When the needle hit him he moved back against the wall. But it was so slow that I swear 'fore God it looked just like the wall moved towards him and he was holding it up. When he finished he took the needle from his arm and handed it to the man. He unwrapped the belt and rolled his shirtsleeve down. He was breathing harder now, and beginning to sweat. He was moving now just like a man in a slow-motion movie. He put his belt back on and buckled it and put his jacket on. He went to the door and flung it open. It was then I seen that it was the rooftop, and not somebody's apartment. The other man all this time had taken his jacket off and was going through the same business all over again. I wanted to go outside to see if Ronnie was alright, but the man was fixing himself so I didn't disturb him. I just stood there and watched. All of a sudden there was a loud crash outside. It sounded like a man falling after he'd been hit with a blackjack. I wanted to go outside and look because I didn't know whether the roof was slanted and Ronnie might fall off or if he'd been hit by somebody and was hurt bad and all this time the man had the needle in his arm with the blood coming up dark red into it then going back into his arm real slow as he went tap-tap-tap on top of the needle, and then he was finished and his belt went on loop by loop and he went to the door and looked out.

'Man,' he said. 'That simple motherhubber done fell out.' He put his jacket on and zipped it up and started down the stairs. I stood aside to let him by.

When I got out on the roof Ronnie was laying flat on his back with his legs up like he was about to give birth. His mouth was open and in the dim light his forehead looked exactly like a window pane after a heavy rain. His eyes were wide open, staring up at the stars. I knelt down beside him.

'What's the matter, Ronnie? You OK, man?'

He didn't move. I remembered right then what I'd heard one time in the Army: *When a man takes dope don't let him pass out or he might pass out for good.* So I slapped him. Hard. He didn't move. I slapped him again. He was coming to. I picked him halfway up by the lapels of his jacket and leaned hang up against a chimney.

'Ronnie!' I shouted, and shook him. 'Ronnie!' His eyes had closed when I slapped him the first time, and now he opened them. He looked like he was trying hard to focus; like he was looking at me from a distance of eighty miles.

'You OK, man?'

'Huh?'

'You OK?'

'I'm awright, Sugar,' he said. (It was the first time any man had ever called me 'Sugar' in my natural life. What the hell, I thought. Maybe he thinks I'm his wife or girl-friend or something. In spite of the situation I couldn't help laughing just a little.) All of a sudden he was alright; or almost alright. He got to his feet by himself. Then he started to slump, so I grabbed him and helped him to the doorway. He shook my arm off. 'I'm straight, Sugar,' he said. I took out my handkerchief and wiped his face. We started down the stairs, and he slumped again. I helped him down a couple flights, then he shook my arm off again. He walked the rest of the way by himself.

When we got to street level he said, 'Git a cab Sugar.' He sat down on the bottom stair and I went out and got a taxi. When I got back he was spitting. I helped him up and he walked to the taxi by himself. As we were about to start off he turned to me and said, 'Did you get your bread, Sugar?'

'Oh!' I said. I'd forgotten my change from the ten dol-lars. I started to get out of the cab, but Ronnie stopped me.

'Lemme do it,' he said. 'That's an evil motherhubber.'

He got out the cab and walked back to the bar. I watched through the rear window to see if he was alright. He was walking just like a man who drinks a lot but can carry his load. In a minute he came back and handed me seven dollars. I thanked him a lot and we drove to his place.

I was sitting in a straight-back chair—I still couldn't take that leopard-skin couch—and he was sitting in the arm-chair. His room-mate wasn't there, and I didn't want to leave him until I was sure he was OK. It was about three in the morning by this time, and I was tired. He had one hand to his forehead, and he was beginning to nod. I didn't want to slap him any more, so I decided to talk to keep him awake. So I talked; just rambling on in general. Every once in a while I'd say, 'You listening, man?' and if he answered I'd keep on. If he didn't I'd go over and shake him and he'd say, 'I'm awright, Sugar, I'm listenin'.' So I'd keep on talking.

This went on for about half an hour. Then he got up and went to the piano. He sat there for a long while just looking down at the keys. Then he hit a minor seventh chord with his left hand. He didn't bang, but he hit it hard and kept his hand there. I could hear it echoing into infin-ity. He hit it again and leaned his head to one side with his left ear close to the keys. Listening. He hit it and hit it and hit it, leaning down lower. His eyes were squinched up real narrow, like he was trying to see the music as well as hear it. It was about then that I seen that what he was really looking at was the leopard-skin couch.

When he talked his voice was real husky, and sounded like he was surprised. 'You know what I see, man?' he said. 'When I look at that couch I see devils dancing in the moonlight. I see angels with skeletons' faces and witches with faces like dogs. And you know what else I see, man? I can see the face of God grinning like a happy nigger.'

He laughed, all of a sudden. Only it wasn't a real laugh. It was kind of a half-crying and half-laughing, as if he'd seen something and couldn't quite express it. Then, just as suddenly, he stopped and got up. I got up, too.

'I got to go,' I said. He looked at me, and his eyes looked just like he'd washed them with some kind of lotion: big and bright.

'Cutting out, huh?' he said.

'Yeah,' I said.

'Fall by tomorrow,' he said.

'I'll be by,' I said. We shook hands and I went down-stairs.

It was warm out. I took my tie off and put it in my jacket pocket; then I took the jacket off and slung it over my arm and walked to the Dewey Square Hotel and went to sleep.

TALISMAN

We'd always thought of Mr George Simpson as being kind of peculiar. He'd leave home about four o'clock in the morning and wouldn't nobody see him before five in the evening. He sported a racoon cap and a pair of knee-high boots, and when it was chilly he wore a lumberjacket. There ain't much more I can say about him, to tell the truth, but I thought I'd tell you what happened one time to him and me and a man named Mr Thomas Love.

One day I went to the drug store to get me some pipe tobacco, and there was Mr George Simpson standing at the counter. Mr Thomas Love, the owner of the store, nodded his head as I went in.

'Hi, Lucas,' he said. 'How's things?'

'Just fine,' I said, 'How 'bout y'self?'

'Not too good. Business been kind of slow.'

'Sure sorry to hear it. I reckon things'll pick up once summer starts.'

'I sure hope so,' Mr Thomas Love said. 'Lordy knows I hope so.'

Mr George Simpson looked up from the can of tobacco he had in his hands and said, 'You got any *Talisman*? This here's OK but I kind of likes that there *Talisman*. It don't bite as much as them others.'

Now, I like *Talisman* myself. Been smoking it for going on twenty years. So I said, 'You got something there. That *Talisman* is real fine tobacco.'

Mr George Simpson pushed back his hunting cap and raised his eyebrows. 'That's what I'm smoking right now,' he said, and looked at me like it was the first time he'd seen me in his natural life. Then, still looking at me like that, he said, 'How's things with you? Got a good crop this year?'

'So far so good,' I said. 'If them weevils don't get to acting up and I gets my fair share of the profits we ought to do right well.'

'No, I ain't got no *Talisman*,' Mr Thomas Love said. Both me and Mr George Simpson turned and looked at him. We'd forgotten all about him for a few seconds.

'You ain't got none, huh?' Mr George Simpson said. 'When you expect some in?'

'The dealer man comes by tomorrow,' Mr Thomas Love said. He looked a lot older than thirty-eight. In fact he looked almost Mr George Simpson's age, and he was getting bald in that widow-peaked way.

'Around what time?' Mr George Simpson said.

'Around six. He usually gets here around six o'clock.'

'Awright,' Mr George Simpson said. 'I'll be here tomorrow evening around that time.'

Me and Mr George Simpson said goodbye to Mr Thomas Love and went our different ways. The next

evening we showed up at the drug store at the same time—
six—and said how do you do.

'Hi,' Mr Thomas Love said. 'I reckon y'all are here for
that there tobacco.'

'I reckon we are,' Mr. George Simpson said. 'That right,
Lucas?'

It was the first time that Mr George Simpson had ever
called me by my first name, and when I said 'Yeah, that's
right' I showed my surprise. Mr George Simpson noticed
it right off and looked away. Mr Thomas Love coughed like
he didn't really need to and picked up a newspaper. Then
he said, like he'd suddenly remembered, 'The dealer-man
ain't come yet.'

'He ain't been here?' Mr George Simpson said.

'Naw. Sometimes he's late.'

'You can't never tell about salesmen.'

'Naw, you sure can't.'

'How late you reckon he'll be?'

'You can't never tell,' Mr Thomas Love said. 'Maybe
five, six minutes. You can't never tell.'

Mr George Simpson sucked on his briar pipe and said
not a word.

'Ho, ho,' Mr Thomas Love sighed.

'Ho, ho, ho.' He sat himself down and yawned without
covering his mouth. 'I sure will be glad when summer
comes,' he said.

'That there chocolate candy you got goes stale when
summer comes,' Mr George Simpson said.

'Do it?'

'Yeah.'

'Ain't nobody ever complained to me about it.'

'I just did,' Mr George Simpson said. 'That chocolate gets stale under that glass case when the weather gets hot.'

'You mean it melts?'

'No, it don't melt. It gets stale and flaky.'

'Ho, ho,' Mr Thomas Love said. He put his thumbs under his suspender straps and yawned again.

About that time a car came up to the doorway and stopped. It was a black van with the word *Talisman* painted on it in yellow letters, with the tail of the *N* curving down beneath the rest. A man got out of the cab—a white man in a grey uniform with the word *Talisman* printed across the chest of it just like it was on the car—and came into the store.

'Howdy, Tom,' he said.

'Hi, Mr Johnson,' Mr Thomas Love said.

'How's business?'

'Mighty poorly, Mr Johnson, mighty poorly.'

'How much you reckon you'll need this time?'

'Oh, I reckon one case'll be enough.'

'Only one?'

'Yeah.'

'Whew!' Mr Johnson said. 'Sure is getting hot, ain't it? Before you know it it'll be summertime.'

'I sure hope so,' Mr Thomas Love said.

'Gimme a coke, Tom,' Mr Johnson said. Mr Thomas Love went to the cooler and took out a bottle of Coca Cola. He opened it and set it on the counter in front of Mr Johnson. Mr Johnson took a swig and said, 'Ah! The pause that refreshes, Tom, the pause that refreshes.'

'Why'nt you get two cases, Tom?' Mr George Simpson said. 'Me and Lucas here will be steady customers, won't we, Lucas?'

'That we will,' I said.

'I can't get two cases,' Mr Thomas Love said. 'All I can get is one.'

'You mean I got to come down here all the way from Birmingham just to sell you one case of tobacco?' Mr Johnson said. Only it looked like he half meant it and half not, in that funny way salesmen have of looking you right dead in the eye and not believing a word of what they're saying. Mr Thomas Love forced a little laugh.

'I ain't the only customer,' he said. 'You got plenty other customers on the way down, Mr Johnson. Plenty.'

'Yeah, but you're one of my main customers, Tom,' Mr Johnson said. 'You know that.'

'Shoot,' Mr Thomas Love said, and laughed for real this time.

'Why'nt you get two, Mr Love?' I said. 'That'll last me and George here all through the summer clean into wintertime. That right, George?'

'That's what I'm talking 'bout,' Mr George Simpson said. 'That's exactly what I'm talking about.'

Just then the screen door banged open and a white woman walked in. We all four turned and looked at her as one. She was wearing a pair of black ballet slippers and a tight skirt and sweater, and you could tell at a glance that she didn't have a brassiere on. She was twenty-four or five, I reckon, and a real looker. As soon as she came in Mr George Simpson said, 'Mmm-*hmph*!', then coughed to hide it. He made such a racket that if you'd heard him you'd have sworn he had TB.

'Ho, ho,' Mr Thomas Love sighed. 'Ho, ho, ho.'

'I thought I told you to stay in the car,' Mr Johnson said.

'I want a coke,' the girl said. She put a forefinger to her lips and bit it. Then, with the same hand, she smoothed the back of her hair. 'Buy me a coke,' she said.

'You get back in that car,' Mr Johnson said.

'No,' the girl said. She walked up to the counter and put a foot up on the railing beneath it. Her legs looked like they'd been moulded by a man's dreams. 'Buy me a coke first,' she said. 'I'll drink it in the car.'

Mr Johnson looked undecided, then kind of confused. He looked away from the girl and then at each one of us in turn, right furtive-like. He put a hand in his trouser pocket and took it out again. 'You get back in that car,' he said. The girl shook her head, and her hair tossed like cornsilk in a high wind.

'Ho, ho, ho,' Mr Thomas Love sighed.

'Gimme another coke, Tom,' Mr Johnson said. His face was beginning to get red. Mr Thomas Love turned around in that slow-motion way he had and got another coke from the cooler. He opened the bottle and handed it to the girl.

'Now you get back in that car,' Mr Johnson said.

The girl walked to the doorway with the bottle in her hand. She stood for a minute with her body pressed flat against the screen, then opened the door, real slow, and went outside.

'Ho, ho, ho,' Mr Thomas Love sighed. 'Ho, ho, ho.'

Mr Johnson drained his coke bottle, paid Mr Thomas Love and said, 'See you all.' We said 'So long.' When the sound of the car had died away I said, all of a sudden, 'Damn it all, Mr Love, you forgot the *Talisman*!'

'It don't matter none,' Mr George Simpson said. 'He'll be back next year.'

LOVER MAN

I'd been away from home for four years. I won't tell you
why I left because I don't think it's any of your business,
but this is what I found when I got back: things weren't
what they used to be. For one thing, Old Man Maypeck
wasn't as active as he was when I left. He'd taken to staying home a lot and when you seen him it was like seeing
the President himself, that rare. For another thing, the
barbershop wasn't never crowded any more. The *po*lice
had took to dropping by right regular-like because of a
razor fight that was held there; and most everybody
thought it best to stay out of sight. But far and away the
biggest change of all was that Brother Jessup wasn't the
Deacon any more.

It wasn't that he was ancient or anything like that.
Brother Jessup was a big, black man, and at the time I'm
telling you about he was forty-seven years of age. He used
to wear a pair of rimless eyeglasses. In church he had the
habit of turning his head up to the light when he talked;
whenever he did this there would be a flash as the light hit
his eyeglasses, and it would look like a pure-T miracle.

Brother Jessup looked like a banker. Even during the week when he wore his work clothes he had the bearings of a banker; but on Sundays he looked like one more than ever. On Sundays he would wear a pair of striped trousers that he got in London, England, when he worked there as a musician in 1929. He had a stiff-collar shirt and tails to go along with them, and he looked mighty good all dressed up.

All he had to say about the entire transaction concerning his leaving the church was two words: 'I quit.' He told this to the minister, who was the Reverend Thos. J. Parker. Reverend Parker was very surprised. When he asked Brother Jessup why he was giving up his position with the church, Brother Jessup shook his head and gave a sad smile; but that was all. So the Reverend Thos. J. Parker passed the word along. As soon as the officials of the church heard about it they tried to persuade Brother Jessup to change his mind. But he wouldn't hear of it. So they got their heads together and decided that if Brother Jessup meant what he said it would be fitting and proper for him to give a farewell sermon. Brother Jessup didn't like this idea a-tall. But they kept putting the pressure on him, and he said he'd think about it.

He thought about it, and decided he'd do it.

That following Sunday night as I was on my way to the church I met up with Old Man Maypeck. You could tell at a glance that it was hurting him something terrible to keep his back as straight as it was. He was leaning on his cane heavier than usual.

'Howdy, James Turner,' he said.

'Howdy, sir.'

'Going to church?'

'Yes, sir. And you?'

'Headed the same way, I reckon.'

Now, Old Man Maypeck hadn't been known to go church for nigh on to twenty-five years. I was kind of surprised, and said as much. Old Man Maypeck didn't say anything for a while; then he said, so soft I could barely hear it, 'I got a feeling this is something special.'

It sure was. I don't know what you would call it, but it sure wasn't what you could properly call a sermon. Throughout the whole thing Brother Jessup didn't raise his voice one time. It looked like nearbout everybody in town was there; but when Brother Jessup started to talk it got as quiet as a ball of wool on a cotton bedspread. This is what he said:

'I'd like to thank the Good Lord for something right here and now. I'd like to thank Him for eyes to look with and hands and arms and muscles to work with. I'd like to thank Him for sleep; both the good part and the bad part of it. I'd like to thank Him for this country and for the fact that there was a white man to think it and a black man to help till it and build it.'

He paused and wiped his face, then went on.

'I like to think that when I die my nigger soul will go to Heaven and not Hell; that when that Day of Judgment comes tumbling down I'll be around to tell the Good Lord that He was right and I was wrong.

'I like to believe there'll come a day when men won't be black or white or blue; but that I'll be Me and you'll be You; a day when there won't be any war no more because there won't be any need for it: Me and You will be One, just like the Good Book means. Then it will be alright to greet a stranger as you would a friend; and tend to his business, too, instead of just your own. I like to believe that one day men won't talk of anything except what's True. That is, of what we're doing here and what this thing called Life is all about. Sometimes I dream of taking a child by the hand and telling him what it feels like to be a man. Sometimes I dream of talking to a woman or a man and telling them exactly what I feel and what I think.

'I like to think there'll come a time when we won't have to eat one another to survive; that there'll come a day when a man will look at a chicken as a chicken and not as Sunday's dinner; that there'll be a day when the dream of all living creatures will come true and a shark will look at a drowning man and nudge him to the surface instead of trying to eat him; that there'll be a far, far distant day when a frog will look at a fly and croak at it.

'I like to believe that the sun that shines on good and bad alike is the same one that shines on things that don't do no good and can't do no evil; that paradise is a place where You can look at Me and know that we are One, just like the Good Book means. I like to imagine that the same woman who wraps her arms around her child will wrap those arms around yours and mine, too; that the Milky Way up above is filled with angels that look down upon this earth with love.

'I don't want you to feel harsh or unkindly because I won't be with you here on Sundays any more. If what I've said here this evening does anybody just a little bit of good I'll be the happiest man in the world.

'Thank you all for listening, Brothers and Sisters, and good night.'

AFTERWORD

When the first American edition of *Lover Man* appeared, in 1959, great pains were taken to make it intelligible to a white readership. A line on the dust jacket—"Stories of Blacks and Whites"—assured white readers that this collection of stories about Black Americans was also, improbably, about them. And in a foreword, the English poet, novelist, and critic Robert Graves advised fellow white people on how the stories should be read and decoded. *Lover Man*, he explained, was a work of "judicious 'signifying'"—in other words, "making a remark about something *un*-remarkable in a situation, and pretending to ignore the main issue." Once you, the white reader, could fathom this diversionary habit, Graves predicted, the observational wit of Anderson's prose would be evident, for *Lover Man* was "the real thing."

What did it mean for a young Black writer to be the real thing in 1959? What did realism look like in Black prose? These questions, untroubling to Graves, were a subject of real debate for Black readers and critics in the moment between the Montgomery bus boycott and the peak of the Civil Rights Movement. The putative realness of Alston Anderson's fiction ran up against the thing he was supposed to represent. Southern and rootless, attuned to new movements in jazz and philosophy, open to same-sex desire, and willfully deaf to politics—these qualities put Anderson outside anybody's canon, and helped to end a brief career shadowed by self-destruction; they also make him a complex case, one whose stories resonate today.

When *Lover Man* came out, overtly political fiction was passé. The scandal of Jim Crow, many whites believed, had been handled by the courts in *Brown v. Board of Education*; all that remained was a few social adjustments for the South to carry out "with all deliberate speed." The plight of the Negro, as such, no longer held the same grip on the liberal imagination. As early as 1949, James Baldwin had decried what he called the "protest novel" for denying man's "beauty, dread, power, in its insistence that it is his categorization alone which is real." By the late '50s, the provocative wartime protestors Richard Wright and Chester Himes had exiled themselves to Europe. Wright had turned to reportage and travel writing, while Himes was devoting his talents to crime novels. Not every Black political novelist went so far away. Ann Petry relocated from Harlem, where she had adapted firsthand observation into the documentary novel *The Street*, back to her hometown of Old Saybrook, Connecticut. A modest move, but from now on protest would be the exception in her domestic dramas and books for young readers.

The most celebrated Black writers of the moment were Baldwin and Ralph Ellison, whose books examined Black identity from within. The subtlety and irony of their novels stood as an implicit rebuke to what they considered the sentimentality and social determinism of protest fiction. Baldwin's 1956 novel *Giovanni's Room* turned its back entirely on problems facing the Black community in order to focus on the inner life of a bisexual white protagonist. When Graves assured readers, in his foreword, that Anderson had "no chip on his shoulder about the negro question," he meant to situate him among introspective writers like Baldwin.

Yet despite his initial acceptance, by Graves and other white critics, Anderson never found a readership that could appreciate his work on its merits. Praised for thin reasons in some quarters, he was greeted with mistrust elsewhere. Baldwin, at least, had relied on the backdrop of protest to establish his bona fides. Anderson arrived on the American literary scene with a book that had originally been published in England (by Cassell, Graves's publisher), complete with British spelling.

What's more, his biography troubled the idea that he was the real thing, if being real meant sharing a background with the Black characters he wrote about. Anderson was born in 1924, in the Panama Canal Zone, to Jamaican parents. He grew up in Kingston, where he attended Wolmer's Boys' School, and, at fourteen, moved with his parents to North Carolina, where he continued his education at the Mary Potter-Redstone-Albion Academy in Oxford. Despite not being a citizen, Anderson enlisted in the US Army in 1943 and achieved the rank of Master Sergeant. His military service took him to outposts in Germany and

Iran. Upon his return to civilian life, he pursued his studies at North Carolina College (now North Carolina Central University), a historically Black institution in Durham, and Columbia University. Anderson then made his way back to Europe, reading in German metaphysics at the Sorbonne. While he made use of these benefits of the GI Bill, his mother Alice worked as a domestic on Martha's Vineyard in Massachusetts.

Anderson's peripatetic youth is reminiscent of the vagabond modernists of the 1920s: Jamaica-born Claude McKay, who landed in New York, Paris, and Moscow, and Missouri-born Langston Hughes, who spent time in Mexico, West Africa, and England. That cosmopolitan spirit might have served the New Negro artist well, but in the early Cold War years it identified the Black writer just starting out as an anomaly. Before he went to Majorca, where he met Robert Graves, Anderson seems to have drifted, artistically as well as geographically. Draft after draft of a novel-in-progress was discarded. He failed to place his fiction with a publisher or a magazine.

Anderson did manage, however, to assemble a transatlantic network of writer friends, including Terry Southern, Mordecai Richler, Ruthven Todd, and Alastair Reid. With Southern he interviewed Nelson Algren for "The Art of Fiction" feature in the *Paris Review*. Todd supported Anderson's application to Yaddo, where in 1955 he spent three months in residence at the same time as Baldwin. But as much as others saw promise in him, Anderson tended to get in his own way. After the fellowship period, Yaddo followed up with a request that he pay his outstanding telephone bill. Anderson declined, citing his financial straits and the fact that he had no time to write. The refusal offended the administration and forever cut him off from an important source of institutional support. When he set out for Europe yet again, it was not out of a principled stand; he was broke.

In Graves, a bisexual, prep-school-educated veteran of World War I, Anderson found both a mentor and a kindred spirit. Yet neither Graves nor the white literary establishment succeeded in explaining, or explaining away, the swerves and feints in Anderson's prose. In the story "Signifying," for example, Anderson's real focus is not on signifying itself but on deeper levels of trickery. Miss Florence is a Black schoolteacher from Philadelphia who is new to the small Alabama town where most of the stories are set. When the men outside the barbershop see her walking down the street, they signify: "What a fine day *this* is!" "My, my, what a *purty* day!" and "I'd sleep in the streets fawdy days and fawdy nights for a day like *that*!" Graves's understanding of the book stops at such good-natured jollity, but Anderson pushes on. The narrator, Thomas Jessup, expects the overflow of rhetorical play, so to set himself apart from his rivals, he deploys "Tactful Approach Number One For Ugly Women," a reversal of signifying that gains advantage by announcing the fact that it's happening. Thomas catches Miss Florence's attention by telling the men to stop signifying because she's "a *lady*." The jiujitsu works, and the young man finds himself in her good graces. But as their connection develops, and as Thomas sees Miss Florence falling in love, he wonders whether a different kind of joke hasn't been played on him.

Lover Man is full of moments of stylistic and narrative indirection, misdirection, reversal, and irony. These features come in a compounding sequence of events rather than a simple twist or turn at the end of a story. The first ten stories, for example, track the dissolution of the Jessup family at a slant, from within the family, *and then* at a remove, as they go their separate ways. Not just signifying, then, but signifying plus an odd or discordant note that alters the whole mood of the story. In "A Sound of Screaming," much goes unsaid between the father, James Jessup, and his mistress after he takes her to have an abortion. When he does speak up, it's to recite the toast "Sam the Man." The effect is both boisterous and disquieting. In "A Fine Romance," the God-fearing Jessup mother, Mary-Jane, kindles a flirtation with a man on the train after locking gazes with his reflection in the window. When she finds herself waking up from a nap, we think it's all in her head, but the man's closed eyes (which Mary-Jane observes are not indicative of sleep) suggest other possibilities. Son Aaron's predicament in "The Dozens" is the most confounding. A day out fishing with his friend Mutton Head turns into tragedy after a dip into the dozens—the verbal sparring associated with "your mama" retorts—glances at truths the two boys cannot bring themselves to utter out loud. The schoolyard taunt of sticks and stones takes on terrible meaning by the end of the story.

As these stories of experience and innocence move, in the final third of the book, from the South to New York City and ultimately the German front, the cast of characters expands to include other Black men spiritually adrift and far from home. When a serviceman befriends an injured dog while stationed in Würzburg, it's difficult to tell whether he is being harassed or embraced by fellow soldiers. A sharp-tongued medic with the outrageous nickname Blackie Brown gives him hell for taking the dog in. Only a delayed indication that the medic is Black himself relieves the tension of the story. In "Dance of the Infidels"—Anderson's best-known story, having been included in a 1965 paperback anthology of Black American fiction—the narrator befriends a fellow jazz aficionado who happens to be a drug addict. While the story introduces readers to the argot of the urban underground through the narrator's wide-eyed perspective, it also spirals into jazz-inflected riffs and one extended solo when Ronnie, the addict, shoots up. That Ronnie is gay and shacking up with a "stud" named Benevolence Delaney, or Bennie, adds yet another layer to the story. The narrator never tells us his own name, but Ronnie calls him "Sugar." Only readers with a taste for this kind of compounded signifying, and with deeper knowledge of the world from which Anderson wrote, will get that Bennie is an intimation of the gay Black painter Beauford Delaney, who mentored Baldwin in his early writing years.

"Dance of the Infidels" is the antepenultimate story in *Lover Man*. From this unassuming position, it might be said to exercise an aesthetic influence over the entire collection. Far from some organic Southern folkway, signifying, for Anderson, is a mode of jazz improvisation, of doubling and doubling back, of repeating with a difference, of swerving from the sound the ear anticipates. (We don't know where Anderson picked up his love for jazz, but a 1947 story from the *New Journal and Guide*, a Black newspaper based in Norfolk, Virginia, credits him with helping introduce bebop to the North Carolina College social scene.)

Bearing that in mind, *Lover Man*, which is dedicated to the avant-garde saxophonist Marshall Allen, may be compared to a jazz LP, with tracks that move to their own beat while contributing to an interconnected whole, and with titles that don't quite name what they're getting at, but instead set an ambiguous or ironic storytelling mood. Riffing on his studies at the Sorbonne, Anderson might contend that there is a metaphysics, with profound implications for Black existence, in the fragmented, frenetic sounds of Dizzy, Charlie, and Miles. Signifying offers readers a way in, but jazz provides the score to those who know how to listen for it.

Few readers in Anderson's time knew how to listen for it, or at least few let on if they did. The mainstream press echoed Graves's praise for Anderson as a writer of dialogue. In the *New York Times*, Selden Rodman described the author as having "a perfect ear, a warm heart, and an amazing capacity to seize character and make it live." Orville Prescott, also in the *Times*, said the stories are "rich with wonderful speech—racy, ribald, robust and startling." The *Irish Times* critic hailed the stories for their "complete authenticity" to "negro life in the American south," as rendered by Anderson's "wonderful ear for the nuance of dialect." Ted Poston, a Black journalist at the *New York Post*, did not deviate from the consensus when he claimed the "unusual thing about Anderson" was "his unerring ear for Negro speech." Behind all such praise was a point that John

H. Hicks of the *St. Louis Post-Dispatch* stated plainly: the book presents "some of the sidelights of a way of life unfamiliar to America's white majority."

If the white press was narrow in its appreciation, Black reviewers tended to focus on what *wasn't* there. Like plot. In the *Journal of Negro Education* Osborn T. Smallwood granted that Anderson's signifying had the power to keep the reader "suspended on the borderland between the conscious and the subconscious." But he faulted the book for failing to build up the "intensity which one associates with the achievement of climax," and he singled out "Schooldays in North Carolina" for not making anything of its doomed "high school romance." For some readers, the lack of conventional plot implied a lack of significance. J. Saunders Redding, writing in the Baltimore *Afro-American* newspaper, contended that Anderson's stories suffer from "a certain pointlessness" and an "adolescent point of view." And why, exactly, wouldn't Anderson write about things that mattered? Blyden Jackson blamed Anderson's West Indian background. In the pages of *Phylon*, the most esteemed Black literary journal of its time, Jackson posited that, as an immigrant to "our South," Anderson experienced American Blackness belatedly and from a distance. No wonder *Lover Man* confined itself to the "pettier concerns" of Black life. Even a champion of the book, the *Pittsburgh Courier's* P. L. Prattis, acknowledged that Anderson's realism was sexual in nature, thus disturbing the sensibilities of middle-class Blacks: "They'll want to say, ''Taint so!' But it is so, and the only reason the bourgeoise will object is because Mr. Anderson has drawn our picture for everybody (including white folks; in fact, mostly white folks) to see." Prattis had no problem ruffling the feathers of Black readers, but he also showed an awareness of the limits of "not pretty stories" to effect change in white readers' minds.

These judgments suggest why *Lover Man* dropped out of sight in the years to come. Black critics might admit Anderson's talent, yet formal admiration could not overcome their disappointment with stories that failed to "achieve climax" in a mature and responsible way. A teenager who cannot get aroused with his girl on the night he says goodbye to his best male friend? Two men who talk a big game between themselves, only to have a girlfriend rebuff their clumsy attempt at initiating a threesome? An anonymous narrator reminiscent of Ralph Ellison's invisible man who acquires a sense of solidity, of self-definition, not from Emersonian insight but from a term of endearment bestowed on him by a junkie? In parlance that resonates today as much as it would have in 1959, the *queer* elements that make Anderson's stories offbeat and bewildering are the elements Black critics thought diminished his vision.

Anderson belongs to that group of writers whom the critic Darryl Pinckney once labeled the "mavericks" of African American literature, those irreverent cosmopolitans who "lived and worked among us without much honor." He was a writer in permanent exile from the group whose experience he couldn't help but represent.

The situation took its toll. A bitter argument with Graves in 1962 cut Anderson off from his most valuable mentor. Drug and alcohol abuse impeded his writing, and

Marshall Allen had to come to Anderson's rescue with financial aid. Anderson somehow managed to pull together the manuscript for a novel, which he published in 1965 as *All God's Children*. An indication of what he really thought of the book is the fact that he wrote to Graves of a suicide attempt around the time of its publication. Suffice it to say that this historical novel about an enslaved man who enjoys an easy relationship with his owners and who, after being shuttled off to freedom, chooses to go back into bondage, left everyone scratching their heads. The high seriousness of the first-person narrator indicated that the book was not intended as parody. It landed with a thud, panned by a few critics and all but ignored by the public. The shift in tone and perspective from *Lover Man* to this nonironic attempt at picaresque may have reflected Anderson's embitterment. If it was substance critics wanted, he would give it to them through the reflection of a funhouse mirror. He looked on with scorn as Baldwin was lauded for catching the spirit of protest. Months before *All God's Children* came out, Anderson wrote a letter to the *Times* taking William F. Buckley Jr.'s side against Baldwin on the topic of civil rights. Now he *was* being petty.

Unfortunately, this seems to be the last published statement Anderson made. After a final letter to Graves in 1966, there is no known documentation of Anderson's life. His death in 2008 in Manhattan went unremarked until two years later, when he was reinterred by an organization that provides military burials for indigent veterans, as a story briefly reported in the *Times*. Anderson left no surviving family members. No one had claimed his body. His vocation, activities, and correspondences for over forty years are a mystery.

After all those decades of silence, this new edition of *Lover Man* returns to us a voice, an ear, that, in 1959, brought a worldly jazz sensibility to bear on Southern Black life. That sensibility was, in its own way, the real thing. Or, a real thing. The qualities that made Anderson sound off-key to Black readers in 1959 are qualities we are more likely to celebrate: quiet modes of refusing the dominant racial narrative of suppression and inclusion. Of unsung Black mavericks, Pinckney writes that "each describes an obsessive's solitary journey and tells a tale of alienated consciousness." Anderson explored the margins of his social world precisely through such solitary, alienated figures. *Lover Man* is anything but what you would expect from a lover man. And as signifying goes, that would be the point.

Kinohi Nishikawa
Philadelphia, 2023

McNally Editions reissues books that are not widely known but have stood the test of time, that remain as singular and engaging as when they were written. Available in the US wherever books are sold or by subscription from mcnallyeditions.com.